Five Children
on the
Western Front

ABOUT THE AUTHOR

Kate Saunders has written lots of books for adults and children. She lives in London.

ALSO BY KATE SAUNDERS

The Curse of the Chocolate Phoenix
The Whizz Pop Chocolate Shop
Magicalamity
The Belfry Witches
The Belfry Witches Fly Again
Cat and the Stinkwater War
The Little Secret

Five Children on the Western Front

KATE SAUNDERS

FABER & FABER

First published in 2014
by Faber & Faber Limited
Bloomsbury House
74–77 Great Russell Street
London WC1B 3DA

Designed and typeset by Crow Books
Printed by CPI Group (UK) Ltd, Croydon, CR0 4YY

A CIP record for this book is available from the British Library

ISBN 978–0–571–31095–1

2 4 6 8 10 9 7 5 3 1

To all the boys and girls
1914–1918

In the old days when death
Stalked the world
For the flower of men,
And the rose of beauty faded
And pined in the great gloom.

> ISAAC ROSENBERG,
> Killed in action, April 1918

'The children were not particularly handsome, nor were they extra clever, nor extraordinarily good. But they were not bad sorts on the whole; in fact, they were rather like you.'

> E. NESBIT, *The Phoenix and the Carpet*

PROLOGUE

LONDON, 1905

'I TURN MY BACK FOR ONE MINUTE, and you're pulling my house apart at the seams! For pity's sake, find *something* quiet to do – something that doesn't break your necks!' Old Nurse looked crossly at the maid, who was giggling. 'Come on, Ivy. Don't encourage them.'

The trouble started when it was too wet for the children to go out. Cyril said that the alcoves on the large, dingy staircase looked as if they were supposed to have statues in them, so he and his brother stripped down to their long, white underwear and stood in the alcoves pretending to be statues, and Anthea and Jane laughed so hard they had to cling to the banisters. But then Robert started doing fancy poses and fell out of his alcove onto the stairs with a terrifying crash, which brought Old Nurse and Ivy the maid rushing up from the basement kitchen.

'So now we'll have to think of something else,' Robert said, buttoning his shirt in the wrong holes. 'Let's wake up you-know-who.'

'He'll be cross,' Anthea warned. 'He'll say we haven't let him sleep long enough.' You-know-who was technically an 'it', but the children had fallen into the habit of calling it 'him' – as Jane said, 'it' sounded too much like a thing instead of a creature.

'I don't care – he should be grateful to us for saving him from that horrible pet shop.'

The four brothers and sisters were staying at Old Nurse's while their parents and baby brother were abroad. Old Nurse (who had once been Father's nanny) lived in a big, sooty slab of a house in the middle of London, near the British Museum. It was a lodging house, but the only other lodger was a grey-haired professor, who never minded about the noise they made – he'd even let them drag him into the game they had with you-know-who.

Cyril was a handsome, adventurous boy of twelve. Anthea, aged eleven, was kind, and liked looking after people. Robert, aged nine, was serious but with flashes

2

of silliness, and seven-year-old Jane was a thoughtful, sharp-eyed little girl who worked hard at keeping up with the others. They were all thin and wiry, with light brown hair and brown eyes. Robert and Jane had freckles. The boys wore suits of heavy tweed; the girls wore white pinafores over their dresses. They were all fond of Old Nurse, but it was sad without Mother and Father and the Lamb (their name for the baby because his first word had been 'baaa'), and that was why they were playing with magic again. You-know-who had a way of finding them when things were sad, or upset in any way.

He had first appeared two summers ago, in the garden of a house in Kent, where they were staying. After that they had moved to Camden Town in London, and briefly met him during another magical adventure with a phoenix. This time they'd found the creature on sale in a pet shop, and smuggled him back to Old Nurse's, where he lived under Anthea's bed in a tin bath full of fine sand.

The four of them squeezed into the girls' small attic bedroom, and Anthea dragged the heavy tin bath out onto the rug. After carefully checking that her hands were perfectly dry (the smallest hint of damp made him feel ill), she gently dug into the sand to wake him.

His eyes came out first. They were on long stalks, like a snail's, and he could move them in and out like telescopes.

'What is it now?' His mouth appeared next, like a little furry funnel sticking out of a pie crust. 'Why can't you leave me in peace?'

He – or 'it' – was called a Psammead (you pronounced it 'Sammy-ad') and he was an ancient sand fairy. The really amazing thing was that he had the power to grant wishes. These wishes only lasted until sunset, which was probably a good thing since they had wished themselves into some very awkward situations. But the hair-raising moments hadn't put them off – as Cyril said, practically anything was better than hanging about before tea on a rainy afternoon.

'We're so sorry if we woke you,' Anthea said, in her politest voice, because you had to take such care not to offend him. 'But we've got a bit of time before tea, and we wondered if we could have another trip into the future – only not so far this time.'

The smooth sand heaved and shifted, and out came the whole Psammead. His ears were large and soft, like a bat's, his round body was like a little fat cushion of fur, and he had long, skinny arms and legs.

'Oh, all right.' When in a reasonable mood the Psammead enjoyed an adventure as much as anyone. 'Bring my carrier.'

Anthea and Jane had spent days making a special Psammead-carrier – by cutting up their party dresses, which Old Nurse didn't yet know about. They were not very good at sewing, but their untidy stitches were strong. Anthea helped the Psammead into his bag and slung it over her shoulder. He weighed about three and a half pounds, and his sandy-brown fur smelled distantly of the hot desert, where he had been born thousands of years ago.

'We wish we could go to the future,' Cyril said, 'but somewhere quite near, please.'

'Very well, as long as you don't complain about it later,' the Psammead said in his peevish, dusty-sounding voice. 'And as long as you leave me alone for at least two days afterwards.'

He held his breath and his plump body swelled up, as it did whenever he granted a wish, until the bag strained at the seams.

And suddenly they were in another place.

The Psammead had taken them to some very strange places. This was quite an ordinary-looking

5

room, however, crammed with old books and statues, and photographs in silver frames. A very old man with white hair dozed at a mahogany desk heaped with papers.

'Well, I don't think much of this,' Cyril said disgustedly. 'I was hoping for an adventure.' Cyril was going to be a famous explorer when he grew up – the sort you saw pictures of in magazines, hacking through jungles and hunting rare beasts. His favourite book was called *With Rod and Gun through Bechuanaland*.

'Look!' Anthea went closer to the dozing old man. 'It's our Professor – only he's years and years older!'

They all gathered round his chair.

'He's so – so crinkled,' whispered Jane.

'No wonder,' said the Psammead. 'I've brought you forward twenty-five years. This is 1930.'

'Crikey,' Cyril said. 'I know we've been in the distant future before – but this is OUR future. If it's 1930, that means I'm thirty-seven years old. Maybe we should go and find ourselves, to see what we look like now.'

'I wonder if I married a vet, like I wanted,' Jane said. She loved nursing injured animals, though she wasn't very good at accepting when they were dead, and had been in trouble for digging them up again.

'Shh,' Anthea said, 'he's waking up.' She patted the old professor's arm. 'Don't worry, Jimmy – it's only us.' 'Jimmy' was the name they had made up for the Professor when he was first swept into the magic. 'We're on a visit from twenty-five years ago.'

He opened his eyes and his wrinkled face creased into a delighted smile. 'More dreams – old age is full of dreams. Hello, my dears. How charming, to dream about those happy days.' He stared into their faces for a long time. 'What a difference you made to that dull old house! The noise and the laughter!' Very gently, with a shaking hand, he stroked Anthea's hair. 'And here's kind little Anthea, who made me eat my dinner!'

'I hope you're better at looking after yourself these days,' Anthea said.

'I wish I could dream you more often. You're grown up now, and it's not the same.'

Jane had started looking curiously at the swarm of photographs. Most were of dull adults in odd hats. 'Oh – I've found a picture of us, but when was this taken?'

It was a picture of the five of them, with the Lamb sitting on Anthea's knee.

'You sent it to me in the Christmas of 1905,' said the Professor.

'Next Christmas – so it hasn't been taken yet.' Cyril frowned at it. 'I look stupid. When it does get taken I must remember not to make that face.'

'It means we'll get the Lamb back, safe and sound,' Anthea said, beaming. 'Just the happy ending we wanted.'

'Happy ending?' the Professor echoed dreamily, as if talking to himself. 'Yes, there were still happy endings in those days.'

'Are there any more pictures of us?' Jane asked.

'They're all pictures of you, my dear – you became my family.'

'I say!' Robert called from the window. 'The street's full of motor cars! Does everyone have a motor car in 1930?'

Cyril hurried over to look; both boys were fascinated by motor cars, and dreamed of driving them. The cars down in the street were long and sleek and moved like the wind.

'I'm cold,' the Psammead announced. 'And the sensors at the extreme ends of my whiskers are simply screaming damp. Take me back to my sand.'

'Don't!' the Professor sighed. 'Don't let me undream you just yet!'

'It's been a lovely visit, but I suppose we'd better go,' Anthea said. 'Old Nurse will get even crosser if we're late.' She kissed the Professor's papery cheek. 'Bye, Jimmy.'

And then they were back in the girls' bedroom in 1905, and the bell was ringing for tea.

'My hat!' said Cyril. 'Did you see the blue one with the open top? That's the one I mean to drive in 1930.'

'Yes, that would be something like an adventure,' Robert said. 'If the future's full of motor cars, I can't wait!'

'I wish I'd had more time to look at the photographs of us in the future,' Anthea said thoughtfully, dropping the Psammead into his bath of sand. 'I saw a couple of pictures of ladies who looked a bit like Mother, and might have been me or Jane. But I didn't see any grown-up men who looked a bit like you boys – I wonder why not.'

Far away in 1930, in his empty room, the old professor was crying.

One

NINE YEARS LATER

KENT, OCTOBER 1914

THE SAND AT THE BOTTOM OF the gravel pit shifted and heaved, and out popped the furry, brown head of a most extraordinary creature. His eyes were long stalks, like the horns of a snail, and they shot out to stare at the astonished faces of the Lamb and Edie. It was a grey, blustery day in October; the two youngest children had come to the large, sandy hollow at the bottom of the garden to escape from the fussing inside the house while lunch was being made.

For a moment, they stared at each other in breathless silence.

The creature's whiskers quivered. 'What is the meaning of this? Where am I?'

'It spoke!' whispered Edie. 'Did you hear?'

'I think this must be a dream,' the Lamb said slowly.

'But I have an odd feeling I've seen an animal like this before – maybe in another dream—'

'I am NOT an animal!' the creature snapped. 'I'm a senior sand fairy – and you have blundered into my sacred sleeping place. Well, it must have been a mistake, so I'll forgive you. Shut the door on your way out.'

'This is our garden,' Edie said, wondering why she wasn't frightened. 'It doesn't have a door.'

'I don't understand. I should be asleep in the baking sands of the desert, and this place is freezing my blood to a sorbet!' He shivered and wrapped his long arms around his stout little body.

Edie and the Lamb stared at his peculiar pucker of a mouth, his sprawling arms and legs and swivelling eyes, and felt a strange stirring in their deepest memories.

'It's the Psammead!' the Lamb cried out suddenly, his freckled face glowing with excitement. 'Edie, it's him – from all the stories!'

'But Anthea just made those up,' Edie said doubtfully. 'Didn't she?'

'I think I sort of knew the stories were real. I think I almost remember the Psammead – but last time he came I was only a baby.'

'And I wasn't even born.' Edie was annoyed. 'Everything interesting happened before I was born. It's not fair. I hate being the youngest!'

'Anthea,' the Psammead said slowly. 'One of the little girls I used to know was called Anthea.'

'She's not a little girl now,' Edie said. 'She's twenty and she goes to art school.'

'Art school? What's that?'

'It's where you learn to be an artist. She draws people with no clothes on.'

'I simply don't understand,' the Psammead said. 'What strange civilisation is this? Why have I shot back into the future? Where on earth am I?'

'I'm surprised you don't recognise it,' the Lamb said. 'You've been here before. This is the White House in Kent – we moved back here when I was little. We're in the famous gravel pit where you first appeared.'

'But – but—' the Psammead's long whiskers stiffened with alarm, 'you're the wrong children! Where are MY children?'

'You mean our big brothers and sisters,' the Lamb said. 'Cyril, Anthea, Robert and Jane – they're all here – and I'm the Lamb.'

'What – you?' The Psammead was bewildered. 'Nonsense, the Lamb is only a baby – a very sticky, grizzly baby, as I recall.'

The Lamb chuckled. 'I've grown a bit since then. I'm eleven now, and I'm a day scholar at St Anselm's. It's 1914.'

'Nineteen hundred and fourteen AD!' the Psammead sighed. 'I swore I'd have nothing more to do with this GHASTLY new century. If you're the Lamb, who is this freckly little girl?'

'I'm Edie, short for Edith.' Edie was so enchanted by the Psammead's cross, faraway voice that she didn't mind being called 'freckly'. 'I'm nine, and I wasn't born when you had all those adventures.' Now that she was getting over the first shock, Edie was starting to realise how wonderful this was – the stories she'd loved so much when she was little had come to life. 'I've always wished I could see you and talk to you, and you're so sweet – may I stroke you?'

'Hmmm.' The Psammead was vain and (as the others could have told them) fond of compliments. For the first time, there was a hint of a smile around the furry lips. 'If you must, but please ensure that your hands are completely DRY – if I come into contact with the smallest drop of moisture, I'm poorly for weeks.'

'I'll wipe them on my skirt to be sure.' Edie carefully wiped her hands on the skirt of her blue sailor dress, and reached out to stroke the Psammead's little round ball of a head. His fur was as soft as mist and as dry as the desert.

'You have a nice gentle touch,' the Psammead said. 'You rather remind me of Anthea.'

'Poor thing, you're shivering. Would you like to sit in my lap?'

'I suppose that might help.'

To Edie's great delight, the sand fairy allowed her to pick him up – he was heavier than he looked, and his body was lukewarm. She sat him carefully on her lap, wrapping the skirt of her dress around his shoulders.

'If you're real and not a story after all,' she said, 'that means the magic adventures were real too, doesn't it? Please could I have a go at flying, like the others did?' This story had always been Edie's favourite. 'When I was little, Anthea drew a picture of me with wings, just like they had. And I wished and wished it was true.'

'They made rather a mess of having wings,' the

Lamb said, grinning. 'Don't you remember? They forgot the magic ran out at sunset, and ended up trapped on top of a church tower. Gosh – to think of that really happening! What d'you think, Edie – shall we make having wings our first wish?'

'Excuse me,' the Psammead said frostily, 'I will NOT be granting any more wishes.'

This was very disappointing – to get the famous Psammead without the wishes.

'But that's not fair,' the Lamb said. 'It's not my fault I was a baby the last time you came – and it's not Edie's fault she wasn't born yet. I reckon you owe us at least a wish each.'

The Lamb was a great one for arguing; Father called him the barrack-room lawyer.

'My dear Lamb, can't you see this is an EMERGENCY?' the Psammead groaned. 'I don't even have enough power to get myself home! For some infernal reason I've been de-magicked and dumped here.'

Far away, from the other end of the garden, Mother's voice called: 'Hilary! Edith!'

'That means it's nearly lunch and we have to go,' Edie said, gently stroking the top of the Psammead's head with one finger. 'It's a special lunch, a sort of goodbye party for Cyril.'

'For Cyril? Where's he going?'

'He's Lieutenant Cyril now,' the Lamb said casually (trying to sound as if this wasn't the most thrilling thing in the world). 'He's going to the war.'

'War? What are you talking about?'

'Our country is at war with Germany. They've got this beastly little tick of an emperor called Kaiser Wilhelm, and they've invaded France and Belgium.'

'Some men from the government took all the horses from the farm next door because they're needed to pull the big guns,' Edie said.

'Hilary! Edith!' Mother called again.

'I seem to have turned over two pages at once,' the Psammead said. 'Who is "Hilary?"'

'Me.' The Lamb pulled a face. 'I'm afraid it's my real name. Please ignore it – Mother's the only person who uses it.' He stood up, brushing his knees. 'You'd better get back into the sand. We'll dig you out again later.'

'Don't you dare leave me!' The little creature was horrified. 'I REFUSE to have anything to do with this freezing damp sand! If I have to stay in this dreadful place, I'll make do with the sand bath under Anthea's bed. Take me there AT ONCE!'

The Lamb and Edie looked at each other helplessly.

'Awfully sorry,' the Lamb said. 'Anthea doesn't keep a bath full of sand under her bed these days.'

'I've told you, I can't stay here. I need someone who knows about looking after sand fairies.'

'We'll have to tell the Bigguns sometime,' Edie said (this was the family name for the four eldest children). 'Won't they be happy to see the Psammead again?'

'Hmm, I don't know about that,' the Lamb said. 'He hasn't exactly popped out at the most convenient time.'

'I could run and fetch them now—'

'They won't believe you.' The Lamb was old enough to know that their big brothers and sisters were far too busy and impatient to listen to stuff about the old stories – especially today, when everything was at sixes and sevens.

'Hilary! Edith!'

'Nothing else for it – we'll have to take him up to the house. They'll have to listen when they actually see him. Can you carry him in your skirt?'

'No, he's too heavy – and his legs are too long.'

The Lamb shrugged off his tweed jacket. 'I'll wrap him in this and carry him in my arms.' He spread it out on the sand beside Edie.

'I don't seem to have much choice.' The Psammead hopped from Edie's lap onto the jacket, and yelped angrily. 'Ouch! I'm sitting on something knobbly!'

'Sorry,' the Lamb said. 'The pockets are full of conkers.'

The Psammead pulled his eyes back into his head, until his face was nothing but a crease of crossness. 'Hurry up – I'm freezing!'

The Lamb carefully wrapped the creature in his jacket, so that not one hair of him was visible. He picked him up and cradled the strange tweed bundle in his arms.

Edie giggled. 'Now it looks like you're holding a baby!'

'Hilary! Edith! Where are you?'

'Come on.' Holding his bundle as tightly as he dared, the Lamb managed to scramble out of the gravel pit, and Edie helped him through the hedge into the garden.

The garden of the White House was a long lawn surrounded by a deep shrubbery, and the two children were able to get to the kitchen door through the dripping branches without being seen from the windows. They halted in the shelter of the nearest rhododendron, a few yards from the back of the house. Mother was on the terrace outside the sitting room, flustered from calling them.

'She mustn't see me,' the Lamb whispered. 'You'll have to create a diversion.'

'But will she be able to see the Psammead?' Edie whispered back. 'Wasn't he always invisible to grown-ups?'

'I can smell damp evergreens,' said the muffled voice of the Psammead from the tweedy depths of his bundle. 'Now I KNOW I'm back in wretched England.'

'Anthea darling, do go and find the little ones,' Mother said.

Inside the sitting room they heard Anthea saying something.

'I've no idea,' Mother said. 'I told them not to go anywhere – Mrs Field will be so cross if we're late sitting down.' She went into the house through the French windows and shut them behind her.

'Good-oh,' said the Lamb. He gave the Psammead

a gentle squeeze. 'Anthea's the exact person we need. She'll know what to do.'

A moment later the kitchen door opened and Anthea came out into the garden. Because this was a special occasion she had left off what Mother called her 'arty smocks' and was looking very grown up in her smart green dress, with her curly brown hair pinned up in a bun.

When she saw the Lamb and Edie scuttling out of the shrubbery she frowned at them. 'There you are – where on earth have you been?'

'We were in the gravel pit,' Edie said. 'And you'll never guess who we found – the Psammead!'

'Go and wash your hands,' Anthea said. 'I can't imagine how you managed to get so filthy. Granny's here and Mrs F is muttering darkly about gravy.'

'Wait – didn't you hear me? We met the Psammead!'

'Oh, Edie – there's no time for those old stories now.'

'This isn't a story!' Edie scowled; a couple of years ago she would have stamped her foot. 'Why won't you listen?'

'We brought him with us,' the Lamb said. 'He's wrapped in my jacket.'

For the first time, their eldest sister looked at them properly. 'What on earth have you got there? Honestly, Lamb – of all the days to sneak in one of your smelly animals.'

'For the last time, I am NOT an animal,' the muffled voice of the Psammead said. 'And I'm most certainly NOT "smelly".'

The effect on Anthea was dramatic and rather alarming; her lips went white and she looked as if she'd seen a ghost.

'What—?' she asked faintly.

'Panther, darling.' Edie grabbed her hand. 'Please listen to us.' 'Panther' was Anthea's old childhood nickname. Cyril's was 'Squirrel', Robert's was 'Bobs' and Jane had been 'Puss', though she'd refused to answer to it for years. 'It really is IT and he can't get home to his temple and he can't stay in the gravel pit and we don't know what to do with him.'

The Lamb gently unfolded his jacket to uncover the Psammead's little head with its soft, floppy ears all squashed out of shape; his eyes shot out on their stalks.

Anthea stared; the colour surged into her pale face and she beamed with astonished joy. 'It's really you

– oh, how lovely!' Her eyes filled with tears and she laughed softly. 'But I mustn't cry, or you won't let me touch you.'

'Certainly not,' the Psammead said. 'Tears are more painful to me than any other form of dampness – but surely you can't be Anthea, you're far too old.'

'You dear, furry thing, how wonderful to see you again.' She scrubbed at her eyes with her sleeve. 'See? I'm as dry as a bone now – I'm going to give you a kiss.'

Edie and the Lamb shot grins of relief at each other – this was the old Panther of the games and stories, and not the serious grown-up Anthea who drew naked people and argued with Father about art.

'Ugh – don't you dare! Kisses are wet, sloppy things – oh, well – perhaps occasionally.'

Anthea leaned forward and gently kissed the top of the Psammead's head, and though he was still trying to look cross, a smile flickered across his furry mouth.

'Now I know I haven't slipped into a dream,' Anthea said. 'But dear old Psammead, why have you come back?' She frowned slightly. 'And what on earth are we going to do with you?'

Two

THE BIGGUNS

'WELL,' THE PSAMMEAD SAID, in a better-tempered voice. 'It's a shame you don't have a sand bath, but I will admit to a certain pleasure at seeing you all again.'

He was sitting in the middle of the rug in Anthea's bedroom, his long legs and arms comfortably folded. The six brothers and sisters knelt in a circle around him.

Edie was very quiet, but her heart hammered with excitement; she could almost smell the wave of magic that had suddenly swept into her life. The Bigguns were so thrilled to see the Psammead that they had forgotten they were big – though Cyril was a soldier in uniform and Anthea a young lady with her hair up.

'Thanks, Psammead,' Robert said. 'It's stupendous to have you back – if only we had time for a wish before lunch!'

'Technically,' Jane said, 'we could wish we had more time – but then we'd have used up the day's wish, and there wouldn't be anything to do with the extra time.' In the days of the old adventures their wishes had always run out at sunset.

'We could wish Granny wasn't here,' the Lamb suggested.

Jane stifled a giggle. 'Lamb!'

'I don't mean dead or ill or anything – just safely back in Tunbridge Wells, and not here, telling us not to fidget and calling us all by the wrong names.'

'Poor old Granny – ignore him, Psammead.'

The Psammead's eyes rolled round to Jane. 'As I have already explained to your baby brother, I shall NOT be granting wishes. It's completely out of the question.'

'I'm not a baby!' The Lamb was indignant. 'And I don't believe you can't do wishes anymore – you had enough magic to get here.'

'We ought to wish for the end of the war,' Jane said thoughtfully. 'But it wouldn't do much good if the wish ran out at sunset, like the old ones used to. Even if we made the same wish the next morning, that still leaves the night.'

'Steady on,' Cyril said, 'I'm not wishing for the end of the war unless we win it – and our army can manage that without magic, thanks.'

'Why won't any of you listen to me?' The Psammead's long whiskers shivered angrily. 'I have just been through some sort of violent magical upheaval. I woke up and I was here – I have no idea why. I only know that I'm not strong enough to get home to my proper hole. I couldn't grant the smallest wish if I tried.'

'You're a refugee,' Anthea said. 'Like a Belgian.' (Anthea and Mother belonged to a relief committee for the refugees who had been driven out of Belgium by the Germans.) 'Well, we're all thrilled to see you again, and you can stay in our gravel pit as long as you like.'

'Hear, hear!' Cyril and Robert said.

'I can't stay in that gravel pit. It tears my nerves to SHREDS.'

The children looked at each other uncertainly.

'You didn't mind it last time,' Robert said.

'That was summer. The sand now has an autumnal chill, very dangerous for a delicate, valuable being like me – the last sand fairy left in the universe, may I remind you.'

'You're even sweeter than the picture Panther did for me when I was little,' Edie said. 'We'll make you another sand bath, and if you slept under my bed I'd absolutely love it.'

The Psammead had been working himself into a state; Edie's adoration calmed him down at once. 'My lodging must be warm and dry and extremely quiet.'

'I'll tiptoe and talk in whispers if you like.'

'That won't be necessary. It's the incessant digging-up I can't bear. Your big brothers and sisters were constantly promising to leave me alone – and constantly dragging me out with their dirty hands when they'd managed to mess up a perfectly good wish.'

'Oh, lor – remember the wings?' Robert said.

All the Bigguns burst out laughing.

'Remember when we wished the Lamb was grown up – and he turned into a horrid young man with a moustache?' Jane said.

'I just wish I remembered it too,' the Lamb said.

26

'And remember when Panther wished we were all divinely beautiful?' Cyril nudged Robert. 'You came out looking like the most utter girl.'

'Shut up.' Robert nudged him back. 'She had you looking disgustingly wet – with long cow's eyelashes.'

'Shut up!'

'Stop it,' Anthea said. 'I do know how silly I was. Now I've come to love your ugly old faces just as they are.'

'Yes, the memories are surging back!' Without moving his tubby body, the Psammead swivelled his long eyes around the circle. 'But dear me, how old you all are! Cyril's a soldier, Anthea is a grown lady – and am I to understand that this lanky young man in spectacles is little Robert?'

'Less of the little,' Robert said, grinning. 'I'm nineteen now.'

'Bobs is at Cambridge University,' Cyril said. 'That's why he looks like a sickening, long-haired poet.'

'I do not!'

'Tragically, that promising little boy grew up to be a four-eyed swot – ow!' Cyril laughed harder as Robert gave him a rude shove, which made all the older children laugh too.

'Shhh – or Mother will hear us and come upstairs,' Jane said.

'And this tall, grave young person is Jane!'

'I'm sixteen now,' Jane said. 'I'm at high school.' She wore a white blouse and a blue skirt, and had a long plait of brown hair and fingers that were always inky.

'High?' the Psammead echoed. 'Is it on a mountain?'

'No, it's a perfectly ordinary school for girls.'

'I suppose you'll be leaving soon, when you marry that vet – what? What is it now?'

They were all in fits of laughter again.

'I changed my mind about marrying a vet,' Jane said. 'I'm a lot more interested in curing humans these days, and I mean to study medicine when I leave school. Lots of people think girls can't be doctors, but that's rot. Actually, girls can do most things boys do, and in the future—'

'Crikey, you've set her off,' Robert said. 'Now we'll get one of her lectures about the rights of women – how the poor little dears should have votes, and sit in Parliament.'

Jane snatched a cushion from the bed and whacked Robert's head with it. 'Beast! Pig!'

'Ow – just like a girl, beating up an unarmed man—'

'Stinker! Poltroon!'

'An unarmed man in glasses—'

'Stop it!' Edie didn't think her elder brothers and sisters were taking this seriously enough. 'We're supposed to be working out what to do with the Psammead.'

'Dash it, she's right,' Cyril said. 'The gong will be going any minute and we can't just leave the old boy in the middle of the floor. Maybe we should get some sand from the gravel pit and warm it by the gas fire.'

'We don't have time.' Robert turned to the Psammead. 'Where can we stow you while we're having lunch?'

'I told you – it must be WARM but not STUFFY, and PERFECTLY DRY.'

'You could hide in my bed,' Edie said, thinking how cuddly the Psammead would look on her eiderdown beside her plush, brown teddy bear.

'Too cold and too smooth,' the Psammead said. 'I might be tolerably comfortable in a bath full of feathers. Do you have any feathers?'

'No,' Anthea said.

'We have feathers inside our pillows,' the Lamb said. 'I'll get mine—'

'No!' Anthea grabbed his sleeve. 'You can't just take the feathers out of your pillow – there'll be no end of a fuss.'

'Good thinking, Lamb,' Cyril said, ignoring Anthea. 'We can take the feathers out of my pillows. I'm going away so it'll be ages before anybody notices.'

'I'm pretty sure the old tin bath from the nursery is still in the attic.' Robert stood up. 'Lamb, come and help me carry it – Squirrel, go and get the pillows.'

They hurried out of Anthea's bedroom, trying to keep as quiet as possible. Jane helped Cyril bring both the pillows from his bed, and his eiderdown in case the pillows weren't enough. Robert and the Lamb managed to carry the old tin bath down the attic stairs without too many thumps.

They had to be quick; downstairs there were sounds of crockery and footsteps, which meant (as Cyril said) that lunch was looming. He slashed open his pillows with his army knife and a cloud of feathers puffed out into the air, making them all burst into yet another fit of laughing.

It turned out that one pillow wasn't nearly enough.

'It's just a thin layer of feathers at the bottom of the

bath,' Jane said. 'And half of it hasn't gone in the bath at all.' She sneezed.

Cyril, enjoying himself, slashed open another pillow. After that he briskly slashed into the puffy bits of his red satin eiderdown, until Anthea's room was a snowstorm of whirling feathers and the eiderdown was a heap of red ribbons.

'I'll try to put it back on your bed,' Anthea said. 'Goodness knows what we'll say when it gets noticed – Psammead, couldn't you manage a small spell so that nobody notices?'

'No.'

'Your fur's full of feathers,' Edie said. 'You look like a snow-Psammead.'

'Or a polar-Psammead,' Robert said. 'The Arctic version.'

'Haven't you finished yet? I'm collapsing with fatigue. And by the way,' the creature added, 'thousands of years ago there were a few of us in the Arctic. Unsurprisingly, they were the first sort of sand fairies to die out.'

The old tin bath was now more or less filled with feathers. Cyril lifted up the Psammead and gently put him into his improvised bed.

'Hmmm, I suppose this will do – perhaps a year or two of sleep will restore my magical powers.' The Psammead burrowed into the feathers and disappeared.

'A year or two!' Edie was dismayed. 'I can't wait years to see him again!'

'Don't take it too seriously,' Robert said. 'He likes company a lot more than he lets on.'

'That's because he's lonely,' Edie said. 'He's the last of his kind in the whole universe – just think how awful that must be.'

Downstairs, the gong banged loudly.

'Phew,' Robert said. 'What a turn-up! Hold on, Panther – you can't go down with your hair full of feathers!'

The Bigguns burst into giggles again as they hastily brushed each other down.

Edie didn't understand how they could treat this crisis as a silly game. She had caught a look of terrible anxiety on the Psammead's strange little face and it touched her heart. 'We haven't worked it out properly. We've got to try to help him – we're his only friends.'

The Bigguns stopped giggling.

'Oh dear,' Jane said. 'I suppose we are sort of responsible for him.'

'We didn't ask him to come back,' Robert pointed out.

'Didn't we? All the other times, the Psammead turned up because we needed him – either Mother and Father were away, or something else was wrong. Well, the war counts as something wrong, doesn't it?'

They were all silent for a moment. Everyone was wondering if the sand fairy had returned because Cyril was going away to where the fighting was.

'I have a ghastly feeling you may be right,' Cyril said. 'In which case, we're honour-bound to help him. Let's meet here again, directly after lunch. Eat quickly, chaps – or I'll be late for the war.'

★

Lunch should have been a solemn occasion. Mrs Field, who did the cooking at the White House, had slaved all morning to make roast lamb and Cyril's favourite jam roly-poly pudding. Granny, deaf and white-haired and (as the Lamb said) nearly as ancient as the Psammead, had come to see Cyril off to war,

33

and though Mother and Father were doing their best to be jolly, Mother's eyes kept misting over, and Father's voice wobbled when he proposed a toast to 'the soldier's return'.

All the six children, however, kept bursting into giggles – especially when Granny innocently wondered where all the feathers had come from.

Cyril was leaving for the local station at half past three to catch the train to London; the hall was piled with his mysterious luggage, which included a real sword and a real Webley service revolver (the Lamb had cut a tremendous dash at school when he'd boasted about this). After cramming down two helpings of pudding, Cyril said firmly that he wanted to say his goodbyes to his brothers and sisters, and they all hurried back to Anthea's bedroom.

Edie immediately ran to the tin bath, to check that the Psammead hadn't suddenly recovered his magic and left them; she was very relieved to see the hump of sand fairy under the feathers.

'I've been thinking,' Cyril announced. He lit a cigarette and leaned against the mantelpiece. 'Bobs and I will be away, and Panther's always busy sketching her naked people or helping Mother—'

'For heaven's sake,' Anthea said crossly, 'stop going on about the naked people! It's called a life class – and anyway, it only happened once.'

Cyril grinned at her; he loved teasing her about the art school. 'The point is that we won't be much use when it comes to Psammead-duty. So Jane, Edie and the Lamb will have to take the lion's share.'

'Good,' Edie said. 'Bags I have him under my bed.'

'I won't be much use either, I'm afraid,' Jane said, 'as I have late classes at school this term, and heaps of work to do.'

'In that case,' Cyril said briskly, 'it's down to you babies.'

'Watch it!' the Lamb growled.

'Actually, it's jolly useful that you two are younger than the rest of us,' Cyril continued. 'You'll have far more freedom to help the dear old Psammead back to his home – or to find out exactly why he's turned up now. And I expect you to write me bulletins at least once a week. We'll refer to him as "Sammy", in case anyone thinks I'm sending mysterious code-words to the Huns.'

'Who—?' the Psammead began faintly.

'It's a name we call the Germans,' Anthea explained.

35

'The Huns were a horrible Germanic tribe in the Dark Ages, so it's not very polite.'

'It's not meant to be,' Cyril said.

'Sammy – I like that,' the Lamb said. 'And if he gets his magic back, you can write us your wishes.'

'I think I'd better steer clear of magic while I'm on active service,' Cyril said. 'And I strongly suggest you do the same. Jane remembers the scrapes we got into with our wishes, don't you, Puss?'

The serious schoolgirl let out an undignified snort of laughter. 'Rather!'

'I'm trusting you to give the dear old thing as much help as you can, but don't let him lead you up the garden path.' Cyril glanced at the new watch on his wrist. 'I'll have to be off in a minute. I wonder if he'd mind me digging him up again?'

'He'll complain,' Anthea said. 'But I think he'll like it really.'

Cyril carefully put a hand into the tin bath. The Psammead sneezed, sending up a cloud of feathers.

'What? What is this? I'd only just dropped off into a fitful half-slumber!'

'Sorry, old chap.' Cyril gently lifted the feathery Psammead into his arms. 'I just wanted one more glimpse of you – it's so good to think about those happy old days.'

'Where are you going, exactly? Is this war nearby?'

'It's across the Channel,' Robert said. 'The Huns marched through Belgium, then they marched into France, and that's where Squirrel's regiment will give them a good thrashing.'

'Yes, and we'll make short work of it,' Cyril said. 'Everyone's saying it'll be done and dusted in a couple of months – I'm jolly lucky to get a look-in while it's still going on.'

'I don't like wars,' the Psammead said. 'Wars are painful and untidy.'

'But sometimes necessary.' Cyril stroked him gently. 'Take care of them, won't you?'

'They're supposed to be taking care of ME!'

'I know – I like to think of you being here, that's all.' Cyril placed the Psammead back in his feathery bath.

They heard the pony and trap on the path outside, and they all fell silent. It was time for Cyril to vanish into the unknown world of the war – perhaps forever, though everyone pushed this thought away.

'Well, this is it,' Cyril said.

'Goodbye and good hunting, dear old Squirrel,' Anthea said softly.

Cyril let the girls kiss him, and shook hands with Robert and the Lamb. 'Listen here, Lamb – you'll be Mother's only boy now, what with me and Bobs being away. Don't let her get too blue.'

'Righto.' It came out gruffly, because the Lamb had a lump in his throat.

Cyril let out a shaky laugh. 'Toodle-oo, Psammead.'

'Toodle-oo? What on earth is that?'

'It's a new word for goodbye.'

'Really? How quickly the language changes! "Toodle-oo", my dear Cyril.'

They had all been rather choked up, but hearing the Psammead saying 'toodle-oo' was so funny that they were all giggling again when they trooped downstairs.

Cyril's luggage had been loaded onto the trap. Mother and Father were waiting in the hall with Granny. Father kept clearing his throat and looking at his old-fashioned pocket watch (only soldiers like Cyril wore wristwatches). Mother was making an enormous effort not to cry.

Cyril kissed her and folded his arms around her.

'Goodbye, Mother – please don't worry too much. I'll be back before you know it.'

'My adventurous boy,' Mother said. 'God keep you safe.'

Mrs Field, who had come out of the kitchen with her husband and Lizzie the housemaid, gave Cyril a smacking kiss on the cheek. 'Take care of yourself, dear. I'll send a cake as soon as you're settled.'

Though he had already said goodbye to his brothers and sisters, Cyril hugged them all again. 'Be good, you lot.'

Edie sniffed hard to stop herself crying; Cyril was so old that she was used to him going away, but all the other times they had known for sure that they would see him again.

'And don't forget to write about Sammy,' Cyril whispered in her ear.

'No point in hanging about,' Father said. 'Don't want to miss that train.'

Cyril and Father climbed into the pony-trap, and they waved until it turned the corner of the lane and disappeared.

Three

A CASE OF MISTAKEN IDENTITY

THE PSAMMEAD SPENT HIS first night in Robert's bedroom (which they had all hastily agreed was the safest hiding place for the moment), his tin bath hidden behind a wall of Greek and Latin dictionaries. Next morning, while Anthea was in London at her art college and Jane, Edie and the Lamb were at school, Robert, who wasn't going back to Cambridge until the end of the week, drove the pony-trap into the nearby town of Sevenoaks and bought several large sacks of fine builder's sand. They had decided that the attic was the best long-term home for their sand fairy; it was dark and draughty and crammed like a jumble sale with crippled furniture and burst cushions, and nobody ever went in there. Robert put the tin bath under a table with a rickety leg and filled it with the soft new sand.

When the others came home in the afternoon and rushed straight upstairs to see the Psammead, they found him sitting comfortably in his new bed, with just his head sticking out.

'Good wheeze, Bobs,' the Lamb said approvingly. 'I was wondering where we'd get more feathers for him.'

'This sand is of a very high quality, and even distantly reminds me of the lovely sand-hole I had in my palace,' the Psammead said. 'I may even get a little sleep tonight.'

'You never told us you had a palace,' Jane said. 'Where was it?'

'It doesn't matter,' the Psammead said with a deep sigh. 'It crumbled to dust long years ago.'

Edie leaned over the tin bath to stroke the Psammead's head; she'd had a niggling fear all day that he wouldn't be there when she got back, and horrible Miss Bligh had given her a black mark for daydreaming during a history lesson. 'I do wish I could have you under my bed.'

'For the last time, you know it wouldn't wash,' Anthea said. 'If Mother suddenly found a tin bath full of sand under your bed, there'd be all sorts of awkward questions.'

'But would she be able to see old Sammy?' the Lamb asked. 'We couldn't remember if he was invisible to grown-ups.'

'If Mother and Father can see him,' Robert said, 'we ought to come clean and introduce him properly right now.'

The Psammead rose a couple of inches out of his sand and said grandly, 'Only the chosen ones may see and hear me. This is the magic that has protected me from the unknowing since the first pyramid was built. My life has depended on this invisibility, and it is everlasting.'

'Yes, but you keep saying your magic powers have gone up the spout,' the Lamb said. 'How do you know your invisibility hasn't gone too?'

'It is deep in my bones, and in both my hearts – for I have two of them, one on each side,' the Psammead said gravely. 'You may rest assured that nobody will be able to see me unless I wish them to.'

They soon found out that he was wrong about this.

The following Sunday morning, Mrs Field went up to the attic to look for a jelly mould, and then thundered down the narrow stairs with such loud screams that Father came out of his study.

42

'Mr P, there's a rat got into the attic – a great big beast of a thing – sitting in the old pram bold as brass!'

'Well, what do you expect me to do – ask it to leave?' Father said. He worked as the editor of a weekly magazine, and did not like being interrupted while he was reading the Sunday newspapers. 'Can't Field deal with it?'

'He's gone to see his mother, sir – and I can't cook when I know there's a rat in the house. You'll have to kill it.'

Everyone was out in the hall now.

Edie tugged at Robert's sleeve, feeling sick. 'Don't let him kill the Psammead!' she whispered.

'I'll take a look,' Robert said quickly.

'Me too,' the Lamb said.

The two boys went up to the attic, pretending to be searching for the enormous rat Mrs Field thought she'd seen. As she said, they found him squatting on top of the old pram that hadn't been used since Edie was a baby.

'Hello, how nice of you all to pop in,' he said graciously. 'Tell me, what made your fat slave-woman scream like that?'

'She saw you,' the Lamb said. 'So much for your everlasting invisibility.'

'Saw me?' The Psammead was rattled. 'The spell must've worn off. I really don't understand this.'

Robert picked him up and firmly put him back in his sand bath. 'You gave poor old Mrs F a dreadful shock – and by the way, she's not a slave.'

'She thought you were a rat,' Edie said.

The corner of the Psammead's mouth drooped. 'A rat? Of all the insults! And so it has come to this.' He was talking to himself now. 'How are the mighty fallen – from desert god to household vermin!' He let out a long sigh. 'If I can't make that masking spell work again, I will take more care not to be seen by strangers.'

Letter from Lieutenant C. J. Pemberton, 9th Loamshires,
23rd October 1914
Somewhere on the Western Front

Dear Anthea, Jane, Lamb, Edie – and a certain 'Sammy',

Thanks for the letter. Poor old Mrs F, Sammy gave her quite a turn.

In my opinion, Sammy will be a lot more trouble if he lets the wrong people see him. They'll either shriek like Mrs F or sell him to a travelling circus, and I can't bear to think of that. Sammy, keep your head down.

I can't tell you exactly where I am in case the Kaiser intercepts this letter and learns vital things about the war. I can tell you that I'm writing this in a khaki tent, on a hillside covered with khaki tents as far as the eye can see. I share my tent with a very decent chap called Harper, who is at this moment lying on his camp bed trying to read a Sherlock Holmes novel by the light of one small oil lamp. It's a pretty good billet, though Sammy wouldn't like the drips when it rains.

Last night Harper and I stood on a little hill at the edge of the camp, and watched the flashes and flickerings in the general direction of the front. It won't be so easy to write letters there, so you're not to worry too much if you don't hear from me.

Keep cheery, and tell me when the universe makes up its mind what to do with Sammy.

Toodle-oo

Cyril

Four

THE TROUBLE STARTS

IT WAS SURPRISING HOW QUICKLY they got used to living with the Psammead. He stayed in his bath filled with sand, and as the autumn turned greyer and colder, and the war in France turned bloodier, the family carried on pretty much as usual.

Their home, the White House, was on the edge of a sprawling village in the Kentish countryside, stretched around a large common. At the railway station three miles away, Father took the train to London every morning to his office just off Fleet Street, where he edited his magazine. Anthea spent three days a week at her art college in Kensington. She was also taking first-aid classes; she longed to help wounded soldiers, like the shattered men she had seen at the station in London when the big hospital trains came in.

'You don't want to stare at them, but you can't help it,' she told Jane privately (nobody wanted to upset poor Mother, so anxious about Cyril, with this sort of talk). 'Some of them have been blown up so badly that there's barely anything left of them to put on a stretcher. I hated myself for being so useless.'

The rest of Anthea's time was spent writing letters for her mother's charitable committees, paying visits to neighbours with her mother, and mending the boys' socks. These were exactly the sorts of thing girls were expected to do in between leaving school and getting married. She worried that she was too busy to spend much time in the attic with their odd little guest.

Jane was just as busy as her elder sister. Every morning she cycled five miles to the high school for girls in the nearest small town, where she had incredible amounts of work and often stayed late; she belonged to several societies and was working the lights for the end-of-term play.

'Sometimes,' she confessed to Anthea, 'I'm just too tired to talk to the old fusspot when I get home – you must admit, he can be hard work.'

The Lamb took a local train every morning to

St Anselm's Priory, the large public school where he was a very junior day boy, and had a best friend called Winterbum – short for Winterbottom, his real surname. The Winterbottom family lived on the other side of the common, in a large red-brick house called Windytops; Winterbum's big sister, Lilian, had been in Anthea's class at school, and the two families were great friends.

When the Lamb came home in the afternoons, he ran straight up to the attic to see the Psammead – but he had homework to do, and war stories to read in the *Boy's Own Paper*. 'I hate to say it,' he wrote to Cyril, 'but old Sammy can be a bit of a bore. The school world is at the front of my mind, and he doesn't belong there.'

It was Edie who spent most time with the Psammead. Her school, Poplar House, was very close by and the day was short. Mother or Mr Field drove her home in the pony-trap each afternoon, and she dashed straight upstairs to dig him out of his sand bath. She loved him so much that she didn't mind the constant complaining.

When he was in a good mood, the Psammead liked to ask Edie questions about her school – which nobody else ever did because they were too old, and too busy with their more important concerns. She told him about the teacher she liked (Miss Poole), the teacher she hated (cruel Miss Bligh) and her battles with the class bully. The Psammead listened very seriously and often gave advice.

'My dear Edie, you really must learn to stand up to this Agnes Foster, who sounds like a very nasty little girl. Couldn't you ask Miss Poole to seat you somewhere else during silent sewing hour?'

Edie found the old, soft baby's hairbrush, and spent ages carefully brushing the Psammead's fur.

'It feels so soothing,' he told her. 'Sometimes, when the wind is in the right direction, I even think I feel a little spark of magic coming back to me.'

Edie was the first to notice that something was wrong.

The Psammead had bad dreams. He would thrash about until the floorboards around his bath were covered with sand, then Edie had to snatch the dustpan and brush while Mrs Field wasn't looking, and sweep it all up and put it back in the bath.

'I think there's something on his mind,' she told Anthea. 'Not just that he can't get home. He won't tell me what the dreams are about, but I hear him shouting things – yesterday it was, "You shall all DIE at sunset!"'

The others, even Anthea, thought this was funny, and whispered it to each other during dinner.

But they weren't laughing for long.

'It can't go on, that's all,' the Lamb said.

Anthea frowned anxiously. 'I don't understand. This never used to happen in the old days.'

'Rather not,' Jane said. 'In the old days, the Psammead had enough magic to keep himself hidden. I can't think why he keeps popping out like this, but the Lamb's quite right – we have to stop it.'

Jane, Anthea, the Lamb and Edie were having a crisis meeting in the dining room. It was early December, and they were also making paper chains for Christmas. Mother and Father were in London at the theatre, and wouldn't be back until the last train. Mr and Mrs Field had gone to bed and it was Lizzie the maid's evening out. It was safe to talk about the Psammead.

'But he can't help it,' Edie said firmly. 'He says it just happens. So we couldn't stop him, anyway.'

'He seems to have lost the power to stay invisible,'

Jane said. 'Or even to stay safely in one place. What on earth will we do if we can't keep him hidden?'

Jane was the first victim. She was cycling to school along a country lane, when the Psammead suddenly appeared in the basket of her bicycle.

'I got the shock of my life,' she told them all later. 'I near as anything crashed into the hedge – and then he woke up and disappeared. Just WHAT is he playing at?'

The following day, during a Latin lesson, Winterbum nudged the Lamb and whispered, 'I swear your desk moved!'

The Lamb opened the lid of his desk, and to his incredible horror, found the furry form of the Psammead snoring gently with his head resting on a pile of inky books. He prodded the creature awake with the end of his pencil, and got into trouble when the Psammead shouted, 'OW – get off, horrid boy!'

'Winterbum thought it was me fooling about,' the Lamb said later. 'So did Mr MacTavish. The only reason I didn't get detention was because he taught Squirrel, and I'm the hero's brother.'

The day after that, Anthea nearly screamed aloud when the sleeping Psammead turned up under a pile of bandages at her first-aid class. Each time he appeared, the Psammead vanished the minute he woke up. He was always dismayed, and always promised never to do it again.

But this morning, just when they were beginning to think the appearances had stopped, they received two urgent letters from the boys.

'Dear Girls and Lamb – SOS!!!' Cyril scribbled from France. 'I was in the middle of inspecting an ammunition dump last night when I found SAMMY snoozing inside a box of shells! For the love of Mike, keep him away from the war!'

'What's going on?' Robert wrote crossly from Cambridge. 'Do you lot have any idea what you-know-who gets up to while you're looking the other way? I took the cover off a dish during dinner in hall – and practically had a heart attack when I found a rather grubby sand fairy comfortably draped around a plate of pork and greens! It's only the sheerest luck that he disappeared before the other chaps saw him. Tell him to expect a piece of my mind when I get home.'

'Bobs thinks it's our fault,' the Lamb said. 'As if we knew how to send him anywhere.'

'I vote we dig up the Psammead and read him the Riot Act,' Jane said. 'He has simply got to understand that we can't look after him unless he stays out of sight.'

'You mustn't be mean to him,' Edie said firmly. 'Whatever's going on, I know he can't help it. And I know he's as worried about it as we are.'

'You spend the most time with the Psammead – I've often wondered what you two talk about,' Anthea said.

'He does most of the talking,' Edie said. 'He likes to tell rather rambling stories, and I can't always hear them because only his mouth and eyes are sticking out of the sand. They're mostly about emperors I've never heard of. And earthquakes and fires. And I think he's worried about something.'

'Well, of course,' the Lamb said. 'He's worried about getting home.'

'I think it's more than that. I think he has a dark secret.'

'What sort of secret?' Anthea asked.

Edie's cheeks turned hot; she wasn't used to everyone staring at her and waiting to hear what she had to say. 'Yesterday, when I went to see him, he was muttering about "hiding from the great justice".'

'Did you ask him about it?'

'Yes – but he got rather shifty and pretended he hadn't said it.'

'Maybe he's a criminal on the run,' the Lamb suggested.

'Oh, Lamb – I'm sure he's not a criminal. Oh, dear!' Anthea looked at the others helplessly.

'Right.' Jane stood up. 'Let's get to the bottom of this before Mother and Father come back. We can't put it off any longer – there's no knowing where he'll turn up next.'

'Bring the dear old thing down here,' Anthea said. 'The attic's freezing, and we'll have plenty of warning if anyone comes in.'

Ten minutes later, the Psammead was sitting in the middle of the dining-room table, in a nest of coloured paper chains. 'I distinctly told you not to disturb me unless the German tribes invaded. Since they clearly haven't, will one of you kindly explain why you've dragged me out of bed?'

They were all uneasy; he was such a touchy creature, and nobody wanted to be the one to offend him.

'Show him those letters from Squirrel and Bobs,' the Lamb muttered.

'Oh dear,' the Psammead said. 'Do I take it that I wasn't dreaming when I visited your brothers?'

'I'm afraid they both saw you,' Anthea said as gently as she could. 'You didn't do any harm – but you really, really mustn't do anything like that again.'

'You can't trust most humans not to treat you like an animal,' Jane pointed out. 'We've already rescued you from a pet shop – next time it might be a zoo, and that'd be a lot trickier.'

'We'd have to break in at night.'The Lamb brightened, rather liking the idea.

'Oh – please do be careful.' Edie dreaded the Psammead falling into the hands of people who wouldn't understand him. 'If anything happened to you, I just couldn't bear it.'

'Look here,' Jane said briskly, 'when you came last time, you definitely had the power to keep yourself out of sight. We were the only ones who could see you.'

The Psammead's whiskers drooped and his telescope eyes retreated into his head. 'I simply don't have the magic. When I first woke up here, I assumed I'd somehow lost my magic by mistake. But the truth is far more awful – I think it has been CONFISCATED.'

'What?' Edie asked.

'It means taken away by some higher power,' the Lamb said. 'Like when Mr MacTavish confiscated my champion conker.'

'But – I'm terribly sorry, dear old Psammead – I just don't understand.' Anthea made her voice as gentle as she could, seeing that the sand fairy was working himself towards an agitated huff. 'What higher power? And why would it do such a thing?'

'Maybe you committed a crime,' suggested the Lamb.

The Psammead's whiskers bristled crossly. 'I'm not a criminal – it's all a misunderstanding. But I can't get home until I make a formal appeal to – to – well, whatever this higher power is that's keeping me here. Don't ask me what higher power, or why it sent me here. The war came or maybe the earth's crust broke.'

There was a silence, and the children looked at each other uncertainly.

'The universe seems to have a message for me,' the Psammead said. 'You must bring me all the ancient stones and carvings you can find lying around the house – nothing on parchment or paper, as that will be too modern. I need to study them carefully.'

'We don't have things like that here,' Edie said. 'They're all shut up inside museums.'

'Then you must take me to a museum.'

'You know we can't do that.'

'Actually, I think we can,' Anthea said. Her face lit up and she looked like a gleeful little girl. 'I've had a brilliant idea. Father wants us to visit Old Nurse before Christmas, doesn't he?' Old Nurse still had her lodging house in Bloomsbury, where they'd stayed nine years ago. 'She lives practically opposite the British Museum, which is stuffed with ancient things. We could take the Psammead with us and kill two birds with one stone.'

'Kill birds?' the Psammead echoed. 'Do you mean – sacrifice them to the gods?'

'No, no – it's just an expression.' Anthea made a warning face at the Lamb, who was snorting with laughter. 'And if we go to Old Nurse's, we should think about talking to the Professor. If anyone knows about the ancient past, it's dear old Jimmy. Let's do it this Saturday.'

Five

AN OLD ENEMY AND A
NEW FRIEND

'I DON'T CARE WHAT YOU SAY, this carrier has definitely SHRUNK.' The Psammead's voice floated out of the folds of Edie's school coat, the only one with enough room underneath to carry him in his home-made sling. 'It's so tight round my waist I can hardly breathe!'

It was a raw December afternoon, and nearly closing time at the British Museum. Anthea, Jane, Edie and the Lamb had been there for nearly three hours, searching for anything that might give a clue as to why the Psammead couldn't get to his mysterious home. They stopped at the top of a dingy staircase, outside yet another gallery filled with things from the ancient world.

'Shhhh!' Jane hissed. 'For the last time, keep your mouth shut.'

'He has to talk a bit,' Edie pointed out, 'to tell us where to take him. We don't know which part of history he comes from.'

Edie had been carrying the Psammead all day – on the train, in the ladies cloakroom at the station, in the park where they'd eaten their sandwiches – and his weight was starting to make her back ache, but she continued to patiently lug him through gallery after gallery. And every time, all he'd said was, 'Too modern! Far too modern!'

'How can ancient Egypt be too modern?' the Lamb wanted to know. 'History doesn't go back any further than that.'

'Of course it goes further back!' The Psammead shot an indignant eye out of Edie's top buttonhole. 'The Egyptians were newcomers!'

'I think my feet are about to fall off,' Anthea said. She was carrying a heavy basket with the remains of their lunch and a box of jasmine soap that Mother had sent for Old Nurse (the Lamb would never understand as long as he lived why old ladies actually *liked* being given soap). 'We must've walked for miles, and seen every lump of stone in the world. Psammead, dear, can't we stop now?'

'Hear, hear,' the Lamb said. 'Those sandwiches were hours ago – I'm famished. And I bet Old Nurse has made a cake.' They had arranged to visit Old Nurse straight after the museum.

The Psammead huffed crossly. 'Selfish boy – I'm searching for a message from the cosmos, and all you can think about is your stomach!'

'He's not selfish,' Anthea said, whispering and doing her best to keep her patience. 'And you might be more considerate to poor little Edie, who's absolutely worn out.'

'I'm all right,' Edie said loyally. 'But it's hard to find what you're looking for when you don't even know yourself. And you haven't recognised anything yet – unless you count that statue of the Roman emperor who still owes you money.'

'I told you,' the Psammead said, 'I'll know it when I see it. Where are we now?'

Jane read the notice above the door: 'Artefacts of the Ancient Near East'.

'Hmmm, that sounds promising – take me in.'

They all rolled their eyes at each other wearily.

'Well, all right,' Anthea said, 'but this is the last one for today.'

Trying to look as casual as possible, the four of them strolled into the gallery. They made an odd group, huddling around the small and strangely blob-like figure of Edie. This gallery was a long, gloomy room, lit by flares of gaslight high up on the walls. The glass cases were filled with ancient statues and carvings.

'More dusty old rocks,' Edie muttered. 'Don't poke your head out – we're not alone.'

There was one other person in this obscure and dusty gallery – a young soldier in a private's uniform. He glanced up when they all came in, but was now busy sketching something in one of the glass cases.

'What a nuisance.' The Psammead's voice floated up sourly. 'Tell whoever it is to clear off.'

'We'll do nothing of the kind,' Anthea whispered, with the first hint of sharpness. 'This museum's open to everyone, and he has as much right to be here as you do.'

'Probably more,' the Lamb whispered, 'because he's a soldier and there's a war on.'

'All right! Walk me round these glass cases and get as close as you can.'

Once again they began the slow shuffle past the exhibits.

'YOU!' the Psammead gasped suddenly.

'You've seen something!' Edie forgot to whisper. 'You're trembling!'

'Enheduanna!' groaned the Psammead. 'Am I never to be free?'

'What do you mean? Where is it?'

'Far, far away, on the banks of the Euphrates—'

The Lamb bent down to read the printed notice. 'The things in this case are from the Akkadian Empire, twenty-fourth century BC – crikey, did the world even exist that long ago?'

'Ow!' Edie yelped. 'Keep still!'

There was a loud ripping sound and before anyone had time to do anything the Psammead suddenly dropped onto the polished floor in a tangle of arms and legs.

Frozen with horror, the four of them watched him scuttling like a fat, furry spider across the floor to the glass case.

Edie hurried after him. 'Come back!'

It was too late.

'Excuse me, Miss,' the young soldier said. 'You can't bring animals in here – blimey, what IS that?'

He dropped his sketchbook on a nearby bench and

came to stare at the Psammead. He was a very nice-looking young man with a friendly face and bright blue eyes, and Edie was glad to see that he wasn't frightened or angry – in fact, he seemed fascinated.

'Blimey!' he said again.

'I TOLD you my carrier was too tight,' snapped the Psammead. 'And by the way, young man, I am NOT an animal.'

The soldier's face was a study of astonishment as he turned pale and his mouth fell open.

There was a long, dreadful silence. Was this the end of keeping their sand fairy secret? Would this soldier call the museum guards and the police?

'It spoke!' the soldier whispered. 'Am I going barmy?'

'Not at all,' the Psammead said. 'You're extremely fortunate – very few people have seen an authentic sand fairy. If everything was in its right place, you'd be bowing and worshipping me.'

'Sorry, chum.' The soldier grinned suddenly. 'I've never heard of sand fairies, and I'm not the worshipping type.'

The Psammead shot out his eyes and took a good look at the young man. 'I see that you wear the uniform of a common soldier, and you speak with the common accent of an underling. I've no idea why the universe has introduced us.'

'I'm no underling, chum. And I'm proud to wear the uniform of a common soldier.'

'Please,' Anthea whispered, her face as red as a brick, 'please don't mind him – he doesn't mean anything.'

'He can be quite rude sometimes,' the Lamb said. 'But only because his brain's sort of stuck thousands of years in the past.'

'Let me introduce myself to this warrior slave,' the Psammead said grandly. 'I am the Psammead – spelled P.S.A.M.M.E.A.D.'

The young soldier stopped looking at Anthea and chuckled. 'You're a proper caution, whatever you are. I'd pay good money to see something like you in a music hall.'

'Now, who are you? Do you have a name – or perhaps a slave number?'

'He's not a slave!' the Lamb hissed.

The young soldier was laughing now, not at all offended but gazing at the Psammead with such delight that it made him look hardly older than the

Lamb. 'I'll give you my name, rank and serial number – Private Haywood E., 2646388. You can call me Ernie. Blimey – if the other fellows in my hut could see me now! They think I'm crazy for spending my weekend leave in a museum.'

Far away, deep in the bowels of the great building, a bell rang.

'Closing time,' Jane said. 'We're miles from the main door. We'd better hurry – Edie, can you get the Psammead back into his carrier?'

'I don't think so.' Edie opened her coat; the carrier Anthea and Jane had stitched all those years ago was now nothing but a few faded rags. 'He's broken it. Now what do we do?'

'You could put him in your basket if you take the things out,' Ernie said.

'Good idea.' The Lamb grabbed Anthea's basket and took out the Thermos flask, the lunch remains and the box of soap. 'We can cover him with the napkin.'

'How very undignified,' the Psammead said. 'It had better not be damp.'

'Let me give you a hand, chum.' Ernie bent down and picked up the Psammead as if he'd been doing it for years. 'In you go.'

The bell rang again. Ernie ran back to the bench to pick up his sketchbook and his magazine.

'Look,' the Lamb said. 'You're reading the *New Citizen*! I'm not bragging or anything, but our father's the editor.'

'Never!' Ernie was impressed. 'Your dad's C. J. Pemberton? I've just been reading his leading article about the Defence of the Realm Act!'

Anthea quickly checked the linen napkin for dampness. 'This isn't the usual sort of introduction, but these aren't the usual circumstances – yes, we're the Pemberton family. I'm Anthea and this is Jane, Hilary, Edith—'

'But everyone calls me the Lamb,' the Lamb put in.

'How do you do,' Ernie said. 'No time for hand-shaking. I'll see you out – let me carry him, Miss Pemberton.' He took the napkin from Anthea and carefully draped it over the hump of Psammead in the basket.

'He thinks Anthea is very pretty,' they heard the Psammead announce.

This time, both Ernie and Anthea turned bright red.

'Do stop embarrassing us, at least for a few minutes,'

Anthea said, half laughing and half groaning (and secretly rather pleased, Edie thought). 'For goodness sake, keep your mouth shut!'

'Come on; I know a short cut,' Ernie said. The gallery was a very long way from the main entrance, but he led them confidently through a door and down a long, dusty staircase that opened onto the darkening street.

It was strange to be out in the busy world again. The street was filled with hurrying Christmas shoppers, horse-drawn cabs and sputtering motor cars, and a barrel organ was playing 'Keep the Home Fires Burning'.

'Well,' Ernie said.

'Thank you so much,' Anthea said.

They gazed at each other, until the Lamb said, 'You've been a brick.'

'Just a minute—' Ernie gave the basket back to Anthea, and reached into his khaki tunic for his sketchbook. 'Before you came in, I was making a drawing of one of those Akkadian stones – look at this!' He held out the drawing, tilting it towards the nearest street light. 'These are lines of slaves, and the scholars think they're bowing to some sort of king or deity. Doesn't he remind you of someone?'

It was only a few pencil strokes but there was no mistaking the long limbs and squat body.

'It's just like him!' Edie said. 'Is that what you saw, Psammead – a picture of one of your family?'

'He shouted out a word,' the Lamb said. 'En – what was it?'

'I can't remember,' the Psammead said sulkily. 'If you don't want me to talk, you shouldn't ask me questions.'

Ernie was excited. 'Was it Enheduanna?'

'It might have been. Don't ask me. That dreadful woman said I had no heart!' The napkin heaved above the agitated sand fairy. 'Complete nonsense, when I have two of them!'

'I just wish I could show him to the gentleman I'm visiting,' Ernie said. 'He's a professor, a leading authority on the Akkadians – his name's J. R. Knight, and I went to his lectures at the Stockwell Working Men's Institute.'

'Jimmy!' Jane cried out. 'That's our Professor! We're visiting him too!'

Six

A VERY OLD QUARREL

A S SOON AS THEY REALISED they were all going to the same place, Ernie took the basket back from Anthea. 'I'll carry his nibs.'

They all walked around the corner to Old Nurse's house. On the way, the Lamb asked Ernie if he had seen any action, and was impressed that he'd been in the famous retreat from the Battle of Mons.

'Our big brother Cyril's a soldier,' the Lamb said. 'He joined the army because he wanted to go out to India – but then the war happened, and his regiment went to France instead.'

'Oh, the front's not so bad when they're not blowing you up,' Ernie said. 'The only injury I've had so far was blistered feet from my boots sliding all over the French roads.' He was more interested in talking about how he had become fascinated by ancient civilisations, and how the Professor had helped him.

'I was born in the East End, where my dad was a docker – the dockers unload all the cargo from the big ships. I went to a council school where we didn't learn much about any kind of history. When I was fourteen I got work in the docks, and then I joined the army as soon as I was old enough. But I went to every library I could get myself into, and I found the Prof's book about the Sumerians. We started talking when I went to his lectures, and he got me a reader's ticket for the library at the British Museum – that's where I spend most of my leaves. He'll be thrilled to meet your sand fairy.'

'He has met the Psammead before,' Jane said. 'But he always thought he was dreaming.'

'I'm not sure I'm not dreaming now,' Ernie said, reddening again as he glanced at Anthea. 'I'd give a year's pay to know what your furry pal's doing on that carving.'

'Slave!' quavered the voice of the Psammead. 'You are jolting my conveyance!'

'Beg pardon,' Ernie said.

'Will you stop calling him a slave?' The Lamb was

getting seriously annoyed by the Psammead's lack of respect for the King's uniform. 'Sorry, I don't know why he's in such a bate.'

'He's tired,' Edie said, as usual flying to the creature's defence. 'This has been a very long day for him – he spends most of his time asleep.'

On the doorstep of Old Nurse's house they lifted the Psammead out of the basket, and Ernie buttoned him into the front of his khaki tunic to hide him; they all laughed softly at the sight of his cross little head sticking out of the collar.

'2646388,' the Psammead said, 'this green stuff is very scratchy.'

'You're right there, chum,' Ernie said, 'but the army doesn't give us nice silk vests.'

Ernie rang the bell. Ivy the maid opened the door, then Old Nurse came hobbling up from the basement and there was a tumult of hugging and kissing. The Lamb and Edie were Old Nurse's pets, and she hardly noticed Ernie, or the fact that they'd all arrived together.

'Can this be my little Lamb? How you've grown – nearly as tall as me! And here's my Edie, quite the young lady! Go on up, Mr Haywood.'

Ernie took off his cap and held it over the Psammead.

'Thanks, Mrs Taylor.' He ran upstairs, past the dusty alcoves where the boys had pretended to be statues all those years ago.

The house was no longer quiet. Old Nurse now let her rooms to medical students, and two rival gramophones were playing upstairs in a storm of thumps and shouts.

'My last two students, Mr Carter and Mr Scott, went off to France with the Medical Corps,' Old Nurse told them. 'Those two young hooligans are Mr Holland and Mr Muldoon – and the idea of them ever being proper doctors makes my blood run cold.'

'That's what you always say, and they always seem to turn out all right,' Ivy said.

'Would you mind if we run up to see the Professor?' Anthea asked quickly. 'Just to say hello?'

'Course not, dear – I've done a good meat tea, seeing you won't get home till past supper time. I'll ring the bell when it's ready, just like I used to.'

On the landing upstairs a lanky young man with red hair was dancing the two-step with a skeleton. Edie squeaked and grabbed Anthea's arm.

The young man bowed. 'Allow me to introduce my bony friend, Maud.'

73

'Muldoon, don't be an ass,' a voice said from an open doorway.

'You mustn't mind dear old Maud.' Mr Muldoon sat the skeleton on the windowsill and dropped a feathered hat on her bare white skull. 'She's had a drop too many.'

The Lamb thought it would be terrific to own a genuine skeleton, but Edie hated its hollow eyes and long claws of hands, and Anthea had to drag her past it.

'Honestly, it's not a person. Think of it as a leftover, like hair clippings or toenails,' Jane said, and would have liked to take a closer look. She often wished she was a boy, so that her parents would listen when she said she wanted to study medicine instead of just saying that women can't be doctors.

In the Professor's large and heroically untidy room Ernie had already unveiled the Psammead. He sat sulkily in the middle of the desk, looking very strange among the heaps of papers and teetering piles of books.

'Come in quickly and shut the door,' he snapped. 'I'm sick and tired of being hidden away.'

'My dears – once again you've managed to turn my entire life's work upside down!' Jimmy gazed at the Psammead, his eyes wild with astonishment. 'You sent me a postcard to say you were coming – but it hardly prepared me for this!'

Anthea kissed his cheek and quickly brought him up to date. When the four Bigguns had stayed at Old Nurse's back in 1905, the Professor had got mixed up with their Psammead adventures, but now he looked enchanted to find that his 'dream' had been only too real.

'You're not seeing things,' Jane said. 'He's back, and he seems to be stuck here. We thought you might be able to help him.'

'That would be an honour,' Jimmy said. 'Look at the carved perfection of his fur! His beautiful dignity! His timeless wisdom!'

The Psammead looked a shade less sulky. 'You strike me as a highly intelligent man. I now see why they brought me here.'

'And you think he saw something in the Akkadian gallery?'

'Definitely.' Edie flopped into a soft chair, which felt delicious after a day of hefting a stout sand fairy around. 'Whatever it was, it gave him such a shock that he broke his carrier.'

'Look at this, sir.' Ernie showed him his sketch. 'You said nobody knew what this figure was – but couldn't it be him? Or one of him?'

'Great heavens!' Jimmy rummaged in the heaps and drifts of paper that surrounded his desk and pulled out a folder of photographs – very dull photographs of old stones in the British Museum. 'The likeness is incredible – well spotted, Haywood.'

Ernie was very much at home in the Professor's room. He hung up his cap, lit the gas ring under the kettle and spooned tea into the dented silver teapot. 'Well?' he asked the Psammead. 'Did you spot one of your relations?'

'No. My last relation was eaten by a Triceratops.'

'So that's you, is it?'

'I suppose it might be.' The Psammead now seemed very shifty indeed. 'You can't expect me to remember – it was two and a half thousand years BC.'

Edie firmly turned the squat, furry body round to face her. 'We've been really nice to you all day – but you've been horrid. We know you're hiding something, so jolly well spill the beans.'

'Hear, hear,' the Lamb said.

'I don't have any beans.'

'Come off it! You know perfectly well what she meant.'

'If you don't tell us what you saw,' Edie said, 'I won't come to see you after school.' Her voice wobbled a little; she hated to think of staying away from the Psammead.

But the blackmail worked; he huffed a couple of times and swelled out his body, and then he collapsed sulkily. 'Oh, all right. It was the carved head of Enheduanna – a very good likeness, in a rough sort of way.'

'What?' Ernie gasped. 'You – you knew her?'

'We didn't get on.'

'Oh, how I envy you!' Jimmy cried out, his eyes alight and his hair all over the place. 'Of all the women in history, that's the woman I wish I could marry!' Seeing their startled faces the Professor blushed a little. 'She was the daughter of the great King Sargon of Akkad, and a high priestess – which in that ancient civilisation was as important as being the Archbishop of Canterbury. And she was the world's first known published poet!'

'Oh, you mean those "Sumerian Temple Hymns" of hers,' the Psammead said coldly. 'They weren't that good. My poems were far better, but they haven't survived because one of my slaves dropped them in the sea.'

There was a silence.

'So you had slaves,' the Lamb said. 'You never mentioned that before. No wonder you're so good at giving orders.'

'I was a desert god and my slaves worshipped me. A few of them died in horrible circumstances, but life was more dangerous in those days.' The Psammead shrugged crossly. 'When that woman became high priestess she had the cheek to tell me I was being cruel to them, and she made a law to set them all free.'

'That sounds nice of her,' Jane said.

'Well, it wasn't – she didn't even pay me for them! I must admit I was furious with her. I cast a spell on her brother and made him dismiss her from the temple.'

'Good grief – she did lose her job as high priestess!' Jimmy was thunderstruck. 'That was during the reign of her brother, King Rimush – but there's nothing in the records about a sand fairy.'

'The spell wore off.' The Psammead's voice was small and tight and hard. 'She got her job back and swore to banish me from the Empire. That stupid Empire has been DUST for thousands of years, but her CURSE lives on, so I've been in exile ever since.'

'A curse! Are you saying Enheduanna was a sorceress?'

'No, but she must have had some good connections. Anyway, I think you'll all agree that I've been treated most unfairly.'

'Hmm, I don't know about that,' the Lamb said. 'By the sound of it you behaved like an absolute cad.'

'My dear Lamb, everyone kills a few slaves!'

'Oh, Psammead!' Anthea shook her head. 'How many did you kill?'

'I don't know. A few thousand. Numbers don't matter.'

'Of course they do! Every one of them was someone's child,' Anthea said.

'But he's sorry now,' Edie said eagerly. 'Aren't you?' She was very shocked that her beloved Psammead had killed so many people, but it had all happened in ancient history, and she was sure he'd changed.

The Psammead shrugged again. 'Sorry-ish, I suppose. If I had my time again I might give them more days off.'

'You're not sorry at all!' This was so outrageous that the Lamb was half laughing. 'We've spent the whole day lugging you about while you complain – and you're the worst kind of bounder!'

'There are certain things that gods do. If you must know, that carving of me in the museum was one of a series.'

'I KNEW it!' Jimmy leaped to his feet. 'Those stones in Stuttgart and Berlin – if I could have just five minutes with Dr Kliebermann . . . his work at Berlin University. Oh, WHY must we be at war with Germany, of all places? I can't get at him now until somebody wins. Never mind the tea, Haywood – this calls for something stronger.'

Edie stroked the Psammead's head; she would have loved to sweep him into her arms, but he was still a stiff little boulder of crossness. 'What are you doing in the other carvings?'

'Committing more murders,' the Lamb suggested. 'Like a furry Jack the Ripper.'

'I am not a criminal!'

There was a sharp rap on the door, as if someone had banged it with a stick, Edie thought.

'Wait a minute – where can we hide him?' Anthea

looked around. It was all right for Jimmy to see the Psammead, but they couldn't risk him being seen by strangers who might scream, or call the police. 'I know, the waste-paper basket.'

The door suddenly flew open on a great gust of cold wind. Anthea shrieked and threw her arms around Edie and the Lamb; Jane grabbed the Professor's hand.

In the doorway stood the skeleton, still wearing her lopsided hat; she raised her bony arm and pointed at the Psammead. The wind grew stronger and shadows began to gather and swirl around the skeleton until they took the faint form of an angry woman with long, streaming hair.

Like a clap of thunder, a voice cried: 'REPENT!'

And then the wind died, the door closed, and the Psammead keeled over in a dead faint.

Seven

A BREAKTHROUGH

JANE WAS THE FIRST TO RECOVER. She ran out to the landing and saw that the skeleton was still sitting where Mr Muldoon had left her.

'Honestly, Edie, it's just a normal skeleton now.'

'The Psammead!' sobbed Edie. 'He's dead!'

'Nonsense.' Jane gave his stomach a prod with her finger.

'Ow!' snapped the Psammead. 'Leave me alone!'

The Lamb was recovering from the cold terror he'd felt when the vision appeared. 'Wait till Cyril and Bobs hear about this – won't they be sick they missed it?'

Ernie took a bottle of whisky from one of the drawers and poured shots for himself and Jimmy. 'Crikey, let me know if you're going to do that again.'

'That repulsive vision was nothing to do with me,' the Psammead said.

'Rot,' Jane said. 'It was everything to do with you. Don't you see what this means? It's precisely the sign you've been waiting for.'

The sand fairy did not look grateful. 'What sign? She didn't tell me anything useful about how to win my power back.'

'Yes she did,' the Lamb said. 'Unless you don't know the meaning of "repent".'

'It means being sorry,' Edie put in helpfully.

'I saw her – Enheduanna, the High Priestess!' Jimmy whispered. 'Just for a moment, in all her majestic beauty!'

'You've got funny taste in girls,' the Lamb said.

Everyone except Edie and the Psammead laughed at this, snapping the tension in the atmosphere. Then the bell rang for tea and Anthea got out her handkerchief and began dabbing at Edie's face, so Old Nurse wouldn't notice she'd been crying.

Jane was thoughtful. 'This is a result – the message couldn't have been clearer. He's here to repent, so he didn't appear because of Cyril or the war. But perhaps they're somehow caught up in his repentance.'

'Stop saying that word,' the Psammead muttered.

'We can't take him downstairs,' Anthea said. 'Oh dear, where can we leave him?'

'Leave him up here with us, Miss Pemberton. We'll entertain him royally,' Ernie said.

'So many questions to ask him!' Jimmy murmured. 'Where does one begin? Haywood, could you take notes?'

Being worshipped like this always improved the Psammead's temper. A smile flickered across his mouth. 'Yes, you may leave me with this scholar and his warrior slave.'

Edie screwed her eyes shut when they went past the skeleton, and they all ran downstairs to the kitchen. Old Nurse and Ivy had covered the table with sandwiches, cakes and sliced chicken, which the children ate as if they had never seen food before. By the time they were all stuffed full, the short December afternoon had darkened to evening and it was time to set off on the long journey home. They trooped wearily upstairs to put the Psammead back in his basket.

'Thank you for being so kind, Mr Haywood.' Anthea shook hands with Ernie.

'Don't mention it, Miss Pemberton,' he said. 'I've had the time of my life – skeleton and all.'

Jimmy absently kissed the girls. 'Goodbye, my dears. Goodbye, oh most wonderful sand fairy!'

'You see?' the Psammead said. 'That is the correct way to address me. Goodbye, young warrior.'

'It's been a pleasure, chum.' Ernie patted his head. 'I hope we meet again. I'll enjoy thinking about this afternoon when I'm back in a trench, with a hundred German shells raining down on my head.' He spoke to the Psammead but was looking at Anthea.

A few minutes later they were outside in the noisy, dirty, bustling street. It was freezing after Old Nurse's stuffy kitchen, and a sharp wind whipped at their clothes.

'I don't think I've ever been so tired,' Jane said forlornly. 'First the tram, then the train, then three miles in the pony-trap.'

'I know, and this basket is dragging my arm off.' Anthea hugged Edie with her free arm. 'Are you all right, baby?'

'I'm so incredibly tired that I don't even mind being called "baby". Oh, I do WISH we could just be at home right now!'

Something knocked her legs from under her, and before she hit the ground, the noise and bustle of the street suddenly switched off and threw her into dark, cold silence.

Instead of the pavement they were all lying on a rutted unlit road. Anthea struggled to her feet, brushing her long skirt. 'It's all right, the Psammead's still safe in the basket. But where on earth are we?'

Jane suddenly laughed. 'Don't you see? It's the bottom of the lane at home!'

It made a wonderful end to the day. They had all been dreading the long trek home, and here they were, with the lights of the White House twinkling cheerfully at them through the bare branches. And more importantly, the Psammead had granted a wish.

The Lamb whooped and punched the air. 'Good stuff, Edie – you made a wish and it came true!'

'I didn't know I was making a wish.' Edie's tiredness had melted away, and she was chuckling softly with the others.

'Lamb, be a dear,' Anthea said, 'run ahead and tell Mother we took an earlier train. She'll be so pleased not to have to turn Field out to meet us that she won't ask too many questions.'

'Righto!' This sudden blast of magic filled the Lamb with excitement. He didn't go on about it but he longed for the kind of adventures the Bigguns had had with the Psammead, and this was the first real sign that it was possible. He stumbled up the lane whistling, making a shortlist of favourite wishes, and wondering if there was a way to involve Winterbum without the whole school knowing.

Anthea and Jane carried the basket between them.

'It's been a lovely day,' Anthea said. 'I'm glad we took the Psammead.'

'Me too, or we would never have met Ernie,' Edie said. 'Isn't he nice? And don't you think he's handsome?' When the older girls at school liked a boy they called it 'having a crackation'; Edie decided Ernie was her first crackation.

Jane giggled. 'Anthea does – oh, you can't hide it from me, old girl.'

'Stop it. I don't know what you mean.' Anthea's expression was invisible in the dark but her voice was smiling. 'He was very nice, that's all.'

★

Dear Anthea, Jane, Lamb, Edie and 'Sammy',

Bad news first, kids – I won't be getting any Christmas leave, as things are busy in our part of the world. Harper and I were pretty sick that we were staying put, but not surprised. I'm counting on you lot to keep things cheery for Mother and Father.

Your letter certainly cheered me up. I wish I'd been there when that ghost appeared and gave Sammy his orders, and I wish like anything I'd been included in that first magic trick; there's nothing I'd like better than to find myself suddenly whisked back home – but seriously, if Sammy's granting wishes again, please don't go making any wishes like that on my behalf. I don't want to be shot as a deserter, as I would be if I vanished from my dugout and turned up in Kent.

We go up the line to the front tomorrow (we're slightly behind the lines now, camping out in what used to be the post office of a village that has now been flattened by the Huns), so it'll be a while before I can send another letter. Don't get too worried, though – the mud's the worst of it.

I spent the whole of yesterday afternoon dragging out a poor old horse who'd sunk into the mud up to his belly. He was thrashing and whinnying and the sergeant wanted to shoot him, but Harper and I refused to give up. He held the horse's head and calmed him down, and the rest of us managed to haul him out with a couple of ropes. We're now plastered with mud from head to foot, but it was worth it – the whole platoon gave that extremely muddy horse a cheer when he was led away.

Happy Christmas! I'll see you next year,

Love

Squirrel

*Postcard from Robert Pemberton,
King's College, Cambridge*

Can't get back till next week, though term's ended – the army's everywhere and they can't find a place for us to sit our exams. I WISH they'd get a move on.

Bobs

Eight

FALLEN IDOL

'I KEEP TELLING YOU,' THE Psammead snapped. 'I didn't grant any wishes.'

'Yes you did!' the Lamb said, through gritted teeth. 'Edie wished we were at home, and then we were. If you didn't grant it, who did?'

'I don't know! It happened by itself and I'm as puzzled as you are.'

The Psammead had been very tired after the trip to London. He had insisted on spending the whole weekend in his sand bath, and Anthea had begged them not to dig him out. It was now Monday afternoon, and the Lamb raced up to the attic the moment he got back from school. Term was about to end, and all anyone could talk about was the holidays. The Lamb had spent most of the day dreaming up the

90

wishes he would make in all that glorious free time, and was very annoyed that the Psammead wasn't even trying to grant them.

'I know what this is – you're still frightened of that skeleton woman who told you to repent.'

The Psammead's whiskers stiffened furiously. 'Frightened – of her? Certainly not!'

Edie was up there too, perched on top of an old suitcase. She'd been deep in conversation with the Psammead and was irritated at the interruption. 'Look, if he says he can't do wishes, you should just believe him.'

'He's afraid old whatsername will reveal more of his crimes,' the Lamb said.

'My dear Lamb, I was a god, and gods don't commit crimes.'

'Stop it!' Edie hissed. 'Leave him alone!' Her school had already broken up for the holidays, and she'd just been to a children's tea party at the vicarage – people were making a special effort not to let the war ruin Christmas. It had been great fun, and only slightly spoiled by horrid Agnes Foster being there too. Edie had been in the middle of telling the Psammead about Agnes blatantly cheating at

'Pin the Tail on the Donkey' when the Lamb came crashing in.

'Oh, I'll leave him alone.' The Lamb stood up. 'He's no earthly use to anyone – all he does is moan! I'm going downstairs to get warm.' Both children were still wearing their coats; the attic was bitterly cold, and they didn't have a cosy sand bath to sit in.

'Nobody understands me,' the Psammead said. 'All you care about is your shallow notion of "fun", while I'm fighting for my very existence!'

'Maybe you should do as the skeleton said, and start repenting,' Edie suggested.

The sand fairy took this very badly; he pulled in his eyes until they were invisible. 'SHE didn't understand either!'

'That's a good idea, Edie.' The Lamb was interested and changed his mind about going downstairs. 'What do you have to do, exactly? In the olden days people used to repent by walking to Jerusalem or somewhere with pebbles in their shoes.'

'That's just for humans,' the Psammead huffed. 'What do you people know about gods, anyway? Oh, the loneliness! I WISH I could talk to another fallen idol!'

A force like strong hands made of cloud and wind lifted them off their feet.

'Good stuff!' yelled the Lamb. 'I knew you could do it!'

And suddenly they weren't in the attic anymore. It was bright daylight and they were in a large formal garden covered with snow. The garden belonged to an enormous and rather ugly grey building with turrets like a castle.

'Where are we?' Edie looked around wildly. 'Where's the Psammead? I can't see him!'

'Don't flap, old thing, he can't have gone far.' This sudden adventure had put the Lamb in a very good temper. 'He wished to meet another fallen idol. This must be the idol's castle.'

'It doesn't look a bit like the castles in fairy tales,' Edie said. 'It's more like one of those big hotels at the seaside.'

'Crikey, I hope we're still in England – suppose they speak another language here? I don't know any other languages. I'm rubbish at French and Latin at school.'

'Nor do I,' Edie said. 'All I can remember from French lessons is "Maître corbeau sur un arbre perche," and that won't be much use, wherever we are. Are we going to be captured by guards?'

'There don't seem to be any guards. I'll sneak a look through the windows.' The Lamb scrambled across the snowy flowerbed to the nearest of the great windows and cautiously looked in. The room was furnished and decorated with grandeur, partly like a fairy tale and partly like the advertisement for Waring & Gillow's that lined Mother's sewing box. The portraits were of people wearing crowns and carrying swords. The room was deserted. 'It's all right, there's no one here.'

Edie scrambled after him. 'No Psammead?'

'No – but this place is huge. We just need to find a way to get inside, then we can make a proper search for him. Whoops – that's torn it. Keep still!'

Through the glass they saw a neat, grey-haired manservant walk into the empty room. They both froze. To their horror, the man walked towards the window. Hardly daring to breathe, they watched as he halted right in front of them – and calmly stared straight through them.

'He can't see us!' the Lamb hissed. 'I think we're invisible! OYOYOY!' he yelled at the top of his lungs and waved his arms wildly.

'Don't!' Edie was horrified, but the man carried on staring calmly. He then turned his back and strolled out of the room.

'This is more like it,' the Lamb said in his normal voice. 'Being invisible was on my list of wishes – though I actually wanted to be invisible at school. And it makes our Psammead-hunt a lot easier.'

'Ugh!' Edie shrieked. 'What's happened to your arm?'

'Eh?' He looked down and gulped 'Cripes!' His arm was buried up to the elbow in the grey stone wall, as if the bricks had turned to sponge.

'Pull it out!' Edie took a step backwards. 'It looks so horrid!'

The Lamb thought it looked hilarious. He tried sticking his arm in deeper, up to his shoulder. 'This is peculiar – it's sort of solid and sort of nothing, like a cloud, only thick and soupy. Is just my head sticking out now?'

'Yes! It's beastly.' The sight of the castle wall with the Lamb's head sticking out of it made Edie's blood run cold. 'Stop it!'

'Wait a moment – this is getting better and better.' The Lamb half stepped out of the wall. 'We don't need to look for a way in now, we can simply walk in through the walls. I've always wanted to do this.' He took a long leap through the curious, soupy cloud, and found himself inside the splendid empty room. 'Oh, Edie, come on – don't be so WET!'

'I'm not being wet!' She was standing beside him on the rich, soft carpet. 'I just didn't like seeing your head all by itself. It looked as if you'd been executed.'

The Lamb passed his hand through a large, yellow satin sofa. 'We're sort of here, and sort of not here.'

'Are we dead?' Edie asked.

'Of course not!'

'We're like ghosts.'

'If I was a ghost I wouldn't be hungry, would I? And I'm exactly as starving as I was in the attic just now.'

This was good reasoning and they both cheered up. It was fascinating to stroll in and out of the magnificent, glittering, over-stuffed, deserted rooms, beneath the blind gazes of huge painted kings and queens. Occasionally they saw a quiet, unhurried servant. Otherwise, all they saw was emptiness, and not a sign of the Psammead.

'If we can't find him,' Edie said, 'does that mean we won't be able to get home?'

'We're inside his wish.' The Lamb didn't want Edie to know that he was worried about this too. 'We'll go where he goes.'

'I'm getting tired. I want to sit down, but if I sit on something here I'll just sink right through it.'

'Look, stop fretting. The Bigguns always got home all right, didn't they?'

'But that was different – they made their wishes on purpose.'

'Stop acting like a little girl,' the Lamb said sternly. 'You're spoiling the adventure.' He wandered through the nearest fireplace – vast and cavernous and made to burn entire trees – and emerged into another empty sitting room.

Edie followed him. 'Funny, I can smell the soot when I walk through fireplaces. And walking through anything is a bit frightening – I can feel it right in the middle of my bones.'

The Lamb stopped mid-yawn and went over to a small table. 'A newspaper – this should tell us where we are.'

The newspaper was called *De Telegraaf.*

'I think that's German,' Edie said. 'We're in an enemy stronghold.'

'It says "Amsterdam" there, and that's in Holland,' the Lamb said. 'Which means this language must be Dutch – my hat!' He suddenly let out a gasp and grabbed Edie's hand. 'Look at that!'

'Let go – look at what?'

'The date!'

There it was, printed in stark black and white – '10 December 1938'.

For a long moment they were both silent, taking in the incredible fact that they were in the distant future.

'This isn't what I expected at all,' Edie said. 'What's the Psammead doing in Holland in 1938?'

'It's a rum place to find a fallen idol.' The Lamb tried to pick up the newspaper, but his hand went right through it. 'It's a shame we can't take this back with us – think how useful it'd be to have a paper from the future!'

'I'd really like to go home. This is a creepy place, even without the spongy walls,' Edie said.

'I told you – we'll find him in a minute.'

They resumed their search through the splendid emptiness – until they turned a corner and heard a familiar voice floating from an open door. It was the dusty drone of their sand fairy in the middle of one of his rants. Edie gasped with relief; she could stand this castle if she knew he was safe.

'My people were very ungrateful,' the Psammead was saying. 'The fact that I kept the streets spotless and built decent roads didn't cut any ice at all! I ordered my soldiers to kill the troublemakers – but they REFUSED! Isn't it awful when your army turns on you?'

'Yes, it cuts to the very heart,' another voice said. 'You are a wise creature.' The voice was old and rasping, with a slight foreign accent. 'You will understand how I felt when my people overthrew me and bundled me off on a train – with practically nothing except the dress uniform I stood up in! And I've been in this poky castle, in this boring little country ever since.'

The children followed the voices into a small, cluttered room, its walls hung with antique weapons and stuffed animal heads. The Psammead sat on a red satin cushion in front of the blazing fire, holding his skinny paws out to the flames.

'Their so-called new government turned out to be a total mess, and I was so sorry for them that I offered to come back – but they said they didn't want me!'

The Psammead turned his head and saw the Lamb and Edie. 'Oh, it's you. I've been having a fascinating time with this very badly treated man, who used to be an emperor. I could talk to him all night – we have so much in common!'

An old man with a white beard and a suit of checked tweed was sitting in a large armchair near the fireplace. When he saw the two children his mouth dropped open and he started shaking violently.

'Hello,' Edie said. 'We've come to collect our sand fairy.'

The old man mumbled something that ended in 'Himmel!'

'You're transparent,' the Psammead said casually. 'He thinks you're ghosts.'

'Transparent!' The Lamb held up his hand, which was disappointingly solid and normal. 'Can he see our bones? Why can't I see them?'

'Because you are guests in my vision. I am solid here because my body moves through time and space with equal ease. Yours don't, so you're not quite here. That's why he can see through you.'

Edie was sorry for the terrified old man. 'We're honestly not ghosts,' she told him kindly. 'We're visiting from the past – from 1914. You might remember there was a war that year.'

When she said 1914, the old man flinched as if she'd slapped him.

'I feel your time tugging at me,' the Psammead said. 'And I'm dreadfully tired – pick me up.'

'No good waiting for you to say please,' the Lamb said. He went over to the cushion and picked up the Psammead. 'Do take us home, there's a good chap.'

The Psammead peeped over the Lamb's shoulder at the old man. 'Nice to meet you.'

And in a second the castle and the fire and the old man melted into a darkness that quickly arranged itself into the attic at home.

'Lovely hard floor!' Edie said.

'Lovely furniture that we can sit on!' said the Lamb. 'I was getting jolly tired of the general sponginess in that castle.' He put the Psammead into his sand bath. 'Who was the old man?'

'I told you.' The Psammead sank into the soft sand. 'He's an ex-emperor. You'd recognise him if you saw him as he is now, because he's a lot more famous here in 1914. Back in these days, he's still Kaiser Wilhelm II of Germany.'

Nine

A CHRISTMAS VISIT

'I MUST ADMIT,' ROBERT SAID, 'when the Lamb wrote to me about meeting Kaiser Bill in the future, I thought he was pulling my leg.' Seeing the Psammead's baffled frown he quickly added, 'I mean, I thought it was a jape.'

Robert had finally taken his exams in the week before Christmas, in the college dairy because it was the only place that wasn't filled with soldiers being lectured about field guns. The college had been taken over by the Royal Engineers, and the shrinking numbers of professors and students had to squeeze in wherever they could. The food was terrible and he was delighted to come home to Mrs Field's cooking. Robert's high spirits had brought a feeling of festivity into the White House, and made the absence of Cyril a little less horrible. The Winterbottoms held a big Christmas party over at Windytops. Robert and his old friend Lilian Winterbottom painted their faces, put straw in their hair, and pretended to be medieval wassailers, until Edie was faint with laughter – Robert, like Father, had a famously dreadful singing voice.

'We've been wondering,' Jane said, 'whether that vision means the Germans are going to lose the war.'

'It does sound promising,' Robert agreed. 'But 1938 is a long way off, and anything could happen before then. Gosh, I wish I'd been with you, to find out what's going to happen to the Kaiser. At the present moment the beastly little man is in charge of an enormous empire.'

'The beard he had in the future looked a lot nicer than that stupid pointed moustache he has now,' Edie said.

It was the evening of Christmas Day, and the children and the Psammead were squeezed around the fireplace in the old nursery, where Mother had said they could have a fire. Jane had put an old cushion on top of the coal bucket, so the Psammead could toast himself near the flames. The day had

been delightful, but it didn't feel right without Cyril
– and they'd had to hide how much they missed him
because it made poor Mother so sad.

'Those Germans should have kept their emperor,'
the Psammead said. 'He told me that the politicians
they're going to get in the 1930s are bandits and
murderers, and frightfully common.'

'I don't see how the Huns could do much worse
than Kaiser Bill,' Robert said. 'If it wasn't for him,
there wouldn't be a war. Pity you didn't shoot him –
except that wouldn't be much good in 1938. Why did
the universe send you to meet him?'

'The universe – or whatever it is – seems to be
reminding the Psammead of his past crimes,' Jane
said. 'We still can't work out why Edie's wish to be
at home worked that time, when none of our other
wishes work. I think it was a sort of hint that magic
had come back to him.'

'I'm afraid those poor slaves weren't the whole of it,'
Anthea said. 'I had a letter from Jimmy. His assistant,
Mr Haywood, had some more leave and they went to
look at an ancient carving in Oxford. Jimmy says if
you read a certain hieroglyph as "sand fairy", it tells
how he brutally invaded the country next door.'

'Mr Haywood is Ernie,' the Lamb told Robert. 'The one who thinks Anthea's pretty.'

'Stop it!' Anthea looked very pretty with her cheeks reddened by the fire.

'Well, I'm glad someone does,' Robert said. 'Because she's notoriously hideous.'

'To get back to the carving,' Anthea said, smiling. 'Apparently this sand fairy burned villages and killed people – just like the Kaiser.'

'All right! Now that I think about it, I may have invaded a small country.' The Psammead pulled in his telescope eyes and his voice became distant. 'So what? It was in the way. That young warrior should stop snooping.'

'He won't be doing any snooping for a while,' Anthea said softly. 'He's at the front now.'

They were all silent for a moment, thinking of the bullets and bombs at the front, and the constant danger.

'I wonder what Squirrel's doing right now,' Edie said. 'I hope he likes the chocolate I sent him. I hope he's thinking about us, and knows we're thinking about him.'

From the end of the lane the wind carried sounds

of singing. It was the local carol-singers, who always appeared at around this time on Christmas night. The voices became louder as they walked up the lane to the White House.

Downstairs, Father had already started to join in the singing, as he always did:

'Silent Night, Holy Night,

All is calm, all is bright—'

Anthea, Robert and Jane smiled at each other. 'I must go down,' Anthea said. 'I promised Mother I'd help her hand round the mince pies.'

'Let's go and join in,' Jane said, 'if only to drown out Father's dreadful singing! Lamb – be a brick and put the Psammead back in his bath.'

The three older children ran downstairs to see the carol singers.

Edie carefully picked up the Psammead. 'Let me do it.'

'It's been a queer sort of Christmas,' the Lamb said thoughtfully. 'If you were still in the business of granting wishes, Psammead—'

'But I'm NOT! As I keep telling you, I don't have power over my own magic anymore.'

'—I'd wish like anything we could get a look at Cyril.'

'Well,' the Psammead said crossly, 'I tried to warn you.'

The soft firelight of the old nursery had been swallowed up in a sea of muddy darkness, lit by sudden white flashes and rocked by constant explosions – some of them scarily close. They were in a narrow trench, leaning against walls made of rough wooden planks.

'Crikey – we're at the front! The actual front line!' The Lamb quickly stood up straight. 'Better not lean on that wall, Edie – I can feel it going spongy. Does this mean we're transparent again?'

'No,' the Psammead said. 'I feel a cloak around us – this time, thank goodness, we're all invisible, just as we were to the castle servants. It means we won't get shot or blown up – though it's horribly DAMP in this trench. Even just looking at all these puddles of muddy water makes me feel ill.'

'My wish was granted!' The Lamb was dazed and his heart was thudding with incredible excitement. 'This is the war, isn't it?'

Edie was so shocked that she felt oddly quiet and

calm; she tried to say something, but her voice had frozen in her chest.

'Obviously this is the war,' the Psammead said, 'but it's being fought very inefficiently. About half a mile away, across the dark wilderness they call No Man's Land, is another trench full of Germans. How are enemies supposed to fight when they can't see each other?'

A series of deafening explosions rocked the spongy ground they stood upon and the air was thick with smoke.

'It's like a firework display with no fireworks!' The Lamb gazed up at the flashing, flickering night sky. 'That was a crump – or it could have been a Minnie.' He had read about all the different kinds of bombs in the war stories he devoured, and now he was inside one, which was terrifying but thrilling.

'Someone pick me up,' the Psammead said. He was perched on a plank of wood that was sinking into the mud. 'Lamb, it had better be you. Edie's touch is gentler, but she looks as if she might start crying.'

'I won't, honestly.' Edie had been on the point of crying but did her best to sound brave.

The Lamb picked up the Psammead and buttoned

him securely inside the front of his jacket. 'And look here, there's no need to gripe at Edie – she can't help crying.' He gave his little sister a rough pat on the arm. 'It's all right, we won't get hurt.'

Edie took a deep breath. She wiped her face with her sleeve. 'Sorry.' The flashes and bangs were terrible, but it helped a lot to know they couldn't be killed by them. 'I've stopped now. Where should we go to find Squirrel?'

There was a wooden door set into the rough wall of the trench; someone had chalked the words 'SALOON BAR' across it. The Lamb firmly took hold of Edie's hand and walked through it. The noise outside became muted. They were in a windowless cellar, where the dim and dirty yellow light came from an oil lamp on the table and oily warmth radiated from a dented iron stove in one corner.

Two young soldiers sat at the table, eating slices of Christmas pudding off tin plates. One had a round, pink, cheerful face and brown hair that stood up like a brush. The other was Cyril.

Edie gave a scream of joy and ran to hug him – but her arms went right through him and he went on eating as if nothing had happened.

109

'It's horrible that he can't feel us!' Edie's tears were welling up again.

The Lamb knew exactly what she meant; it was rather horrible to see Cyril without being seen by him. 'But at least we know he's safe,' he said stoutly. 'And getting a decent-looking pudding.'

'I suppose so. I wish we could tell Mother he's wearing the scarf she knitted for him.'

'The other chap must be Harper – funny that we know such a lot about him yet this is the first time we've actually seen him.'

'Harper?' The Psammead twitched impatiently inside the Lamb's jacket. 'Who?'

'You'd know if you paid more attention to Squirrel's letters,' Edie said. 'He likes cricket and strawberry jam.'

'Of course,' the Psammead said. 'Mr Harper – he has a twin sister called Mabel, and they both have double-jointed thumbs. You see, I was paying attention.'

'This pudding's stupendous,' Cyril said, 'but it's like digesting a cannonball. I may never be able to move again.'

'Careful how you bite it – my sister put in a silver threepenny bit,' Harper said.

'In my family it's a sixpence.' Cyril poured red wine into their tin mugs. 'Cheers.'

'Cheers.' Harper leaned back in his chair. 'I wonder what they're doing at home?'

'I know exactly what my lot will be doing right now.'

'Oh no you don't!' said the Lamb, and he and Edie giggled.

Cyril's voice was wistful. 'The local carol-singers will be making a daring attack, but Dad will be fighting them off with the worst singing you've ever heard.'

'Yes, the singing of your father is frightful,' the Psammead agreed. 'When I heard it on the landing the other day, it reminded me of the death rattle of a mammoth.'

The two young officers were both smiling dreamily over their wine.

'Our house will be overrun with cousins,' Harper said. 'They'll be rolling back the sitting-room rug now, ready for dancing, and winding up the gramophone. That's normally my job, due to my two left feet. I wonder who's doing it this year?'

'The little ones will be going up to bed now,' Cyril

said. 'Arguing all the way, of course. My smallest brother never takes bedtime lying down.'

'That's because it's plain stupid to send a chap to bed when he's not tired,' the Lamb said. 'Especially on Christmas Day!'

Cyril chuckled, as if he had heard. 'Funny, I can see those two so clearly in my mind's eye.' He reached into his pocket for his wallet. 'I've got a snap of them.'

He showed Harper the photograph Father had taken last winter, of the Lamb and Edie with their giant snowman. Father had written on the back, 'All their own work! Lamb, Edie and snowman, Jan 1914.'

'Jolly little cubs,' Harper said. 'I bet they lead you a dance.' He reached for his own wallet and carefully pulled out a small photograph. 'My parents and Mabel – and Hamish.'

'That's their little black Scottie dog,' Edie said, looking over Cyril's shoulder at the picture. 'Isn't he sweet?'

'My father gave me this photo just before I left,' Cyril said. 'He told me to look at it if I ever forgot what I was fighting for.'

They were quiet for a long moment, listening to the pounding of the guns along the line.

'I don't care if he can't feel me,' Edie said. 'I'm going to hug him anyway.' She put her arms around him as best she could and kissed the air near his face. 'Merry Christmas, dear good old Squirrel!'

Cyril grinned suddenly. 'Tell you what, let's drink a Christmas toast to everyone at home.'

'A splendid idea.' Harper held up his mug. 'Here's to Mother, Dad, Mabel, Hamish and the whole dear old boiling lot of them!'

'To Mother and Father, Anthea, Bobs, Jane, Lamb and Edie,' said Cyril. 'And Sammy.'

'Well, I am most gratified!' The Psammead was so pleased to be toasted that he swelled importantly inside the Lamb's jacket. 'I don't have my full power, but I'm sending out very strong vibrations of goodwill.'

'I can feel them!' the Lamb said. 'You're shaking like a little machine – don't burst off my buttons.'

There was a loud knock at the door and a man in a balaclava and tin hat stuck his head inside.

'Beg pardon, Mr Harper – you speak German, don't you?'

'A bit,' Harper said.

'The Huns are giving us Merry Christmas, and we'd like to return the compliment.'

'Crikey,' Cyril said. 'Wonders will never cease!'

The Lamb and Edie followed them out of the dugout. The trench was now packed with soldiers, all grinning. The sky flashed above them as the great guns boomed, but the machine guns had gone quiet.

'Shh – there it is again!' someone said.

Far away in the darkness, voices chorused, 'MERRY CHRISTMAS, TOMMY!'

A murmur went along the trench. 'Go on, Mr Harper!'

'I don't suppose there's any harm in shouting back,' Harper said. He climbed the ladder up to the machine gun in its nest of sandbags and yelled at the top of his voice, 'FROHLICHE WEIHNACHTEN, FRITZ!'

From the German lines they heard the sound of cheering.

★

And they were back in the solid warmth and quiet of the nursery at home, listening to the carol-singers downstairs.

114

'Peace on earth and mercy mild,' the Psammead said. 'You humans are always going on about peace – but if you liked it that much, you'd have more of it.'

Ten

BELIEVING IN FAIRIES

1915

ANTHEA, ROBERT AND JANE were annoyed that they hadn't been included in the magical visit to Cyril. For the first few days after Christmas all the children debated furiously about whether to tell Cyril that they'd seen him. The girls thought he would be pleased, but Robert and the Lamb were dead against it. Eventually, during a cold supper in the dining room while their parents and the servants were out, the boys won the argument.

'We don't want him to think we're spying on him,' the Lamb said firmly. 'It makes me feel like a sneak.'

'Hear, hear,' Robert said. 'I do wish I'd had a glimpse of good old Squirrel – but I might be seeing the war for myself soon enough, if it goes on much longer.'

They were all quiet for a moment. Cyril was a

soldier, strong enough to take on any number of Germans. And though Robert had said he wanted to be a soldier when he was a little boy, he'd grown up into a lanky, weedy, bookish young man who wore glasses, and nobody could imagine him on the front line.

He saw their faces and quickly added, 'Not that I'm thinking of joining up yet – I'm going to finish my exams first, and the war might be over by then.'

The war was spreading across everyday life like a khaki stain; soldiers milled on the streets and crowded the pubs and trains; Father's train into London was constantly being 'beggared about with' whenever there was a big movement of troops. He said you always knew when there had been heavy action at the front because of the long lines of khaki ambulances streaming out of the big London stations and bringing the traffic to a standstill. Suddenly all the young men had gone, and Mother couldn't get anyone to mend the gutter.

In spite of the war, however, a lot of things carried on as if everything was normal. In the first frosty days of 1915, Father's cousin Geraldine treated them to a trip to the theatre to see *Peter Pan*. Cousin Geraldine was great fun and her outings were lavish. She took a whole box at the Coliseum, and when Mother clucked about the expense, she just laughed, and said, 'I don't have any kids of my own – so I can't see *Peter Pan* unless I borrow yours.' She was also good for chocolates and lemonade in the interval.

'I still don't understand,' the Psammead said, 'precisely what you are going to see. Is it a form of worship, like going to church?'

'No – certainly not! The theatre is heaps nicer than church. Everyone wears their prettiest clothes.' Edie had been trying to explain the outing to him for days. 'I'll be wearing my white party dress and my coral locket.'

'I have to wear my school suit,' the Lamb said, 'but it's worth it. *Peter Pan* is a topping play – it's about a boy who wouldn't grow up, and he can fly.'

'It must be difficult to find flying actors,' the Psammead said.

The Lamb gave a snort of laughter. 'They fly on wires and it looks like the most ripping fun. There are also pirates and red Indians, a gang of Lost Boys—'

'And a fairy,' Edie said. 'But she's just a light – you don't really see her.'

'How feeble!' The Psammead yawned (Edie thought the Psammead's yawns, when his mouth went from horizontal to vertical, awfully sweet). 'I must get back to sleep – I'm utterly exhausted.'

He had complained a lot about being very tired after their visit to Cyril, and Edie was worried about him. He was too weak for long conversations and he was having bad dreams again, but she was having trouble making the others take her worries seriously. As usual, she was the person who spent most time with him. The Lamb had got a new and splendid bicycle for Christmas, and he was busy cycling around the countryside with Winterbum. Jane and Robert were swotting for exams and buried in books. Anthea's art college had been turned into a hospital for wounded officers, and she had thrown herself into extra first-aid classes. Edie thought they were hard-hearted. The Lamb said the Psammead was 'just sulking' because he didn't want to repent, but Edie saw bewilderment in his drooping eyes, and lurking terror.

'I need more strength,' he said sadly. 'A little of my power goes every day, and every day I get a little weaker.'

'When Mother thinks I look tired,' Edie said, 'she

gives me Benger's Food. But that wouldn't be much use to a sand fairy. Do you ever eat anything?'

'Not for thousands of years, and then it was only sand. Have a nice time at the amphitheatre,' he said and sank into his bath. 'I hope your chariot wins.'

'He's so tired he thinks this is ancient Rome,' Edie sighed to Jane when they were getting ready to go out. 'He's never been muddle-headed like this before. Suppose he's ill? Would we call the doctor or the vet?'

'I've told you,' Jane said briskly, tying a ribbon around the end of her long plait. 'He's perfectly fine – I listened to both his hearts, and his temperature's normal. I'm sure he'll perk up. You mustn't let him spoil a splendiferous evening.'

Robert and Anthea couldn't come to the theatre; Anthea said she was too old for *Peter Pan*, anyway. The party was made up of Jane, Edie and the Lamb, besides Cousin Geraldine and Mother and Father.

'I'll never be too old for *Peter Pan*,' Father said as they were shown into their box at the theatre, with its velvet chairs and fascinating view of the stage. 'Good grief, Gerry – what on earth are you wearing?'

Cousin Geraldine was wrapped in a rich, fur stole; it was beautifully soft and smelled of roses, though it was rather spoiled, in Edie's opinion, by being decorated with the dangling heads and paws of little creatures.

'They look like weasels,' Father said. 'I feel like attacking them with a broom – do they bite?'

Cousin Geraldine laughed and draped the fur over the arm of her seat – only a few inches away from Edie. Then the music started and the lights in the theatre went down, and Edie forgot about everything else.

Peter was played by a famous actress, who was lovely but rather bosomy for a little boy. However, it was easy to ignore this in the dazzlement of the powerful stage lights and the excitement of seeing Peter and the children flying off to Neverland – 'Second star to the right and straight on till morning!'

It was even better when the Lost Boys (played by genuine children) appeared, soon followed by the high drama of poor Tootles shooting the Wendybird with his bow and arrow.

It was after the interval that Edie saw something move beside her. She looked at Cousin Geraldine's fur stole – and only just managed not to squeak aloud with shock. One of the dangling dead creatures had changed into a stout, brown sand fairy, now fast asleep on the floor. She nudged the Lamb, in the chair next to her. The Lamb nudged Jane on his other side.

They all shot each other looks of alarm and mouthed at each other, 'What shall we do?'

The Psammead couldn't be got rid of unless woken up, and they daren't risk waking him in a crowded theatre, right under the noses of their parents. Edie carefully nudged her foot closer to him, so she could feel what he was doing.

Nothing strange happened until the moment Tinkerbell the fairy was dying, and Peter asked the audience to 'Clap your hands if you believe in fairies!'

Jane, the Lamb and Edie clapped harder than anyone – as the Lamb said in Edie's ear, 'Impossible not to believe in fairies when you've got one sitting on your foot!'

What happened next almost knocked them out of their seats with shock. A huge voice rang through the theatre, loud as thunder: 'NOT ENOUGH! CLAP HARDER! BELIEVE MORE!'

Amazingly, no one else in the theatre noticed anything strange, but they clapped and cheered so loudly that Edie covered her ears. Mother, Father and

Cousin Geraldine clapped and roared and stamped their feet.

'MORE! MORE!' boomed the voice.

It went on and on, until the whole building shook.

And then it stopped, and the play carried on as if nothing had happened.

'What's the matter, darling?' Cousin Geraldine leaned over to put her arm around Edie. 'Don't you believe in fairies?'

Her fur stole, with its dangling dead animals, dropped to the floor. She bent to pick it up, and Edie's heart was in her mouth – but Cousin Geraldine didn't find the Psammead because, mercifully, he wasn't there.

'He's gone!' Edie whispered to the others, and they all sighed with relief.

The rest of the evening passed without incident. They enjoyed the play, took a cab to the station and then the train back to Kent, where Field waited with the pony-trap. It was very late by the time they got home to the White House, and they were all supposed to go straight to bed.

But, of course, Jane, the Lamb and Edie immediately dashed up to the attic.

'I want to see that he's still there and all right,' Edie said, 'but we mustn't disturb him.'

'I'd like an explanation,' Jane said. 'That wasn't ordinary clapping – I thought the roof was going to cave in. And Mother and Father didn't notice a thing.'

'He'll be too tired and weak—' Edie began.

In the candlelight they saw the Psammead sitting in the middle of his sand bath, looking anything but weak – he seemed decidedly pleased with himself.

'That was marvellous – it's made a new fairy of me!' He was plump and sleek, his fur shone, and his telescope eyes bounced about like springs. 'Let me tell you about the fearful and solemn experience I have been through.'

'Not before I tell you about ours.' The Lamb spoke quietly but with extreme firmness. 'Look here, Psammead, I thought we'd settled these surprise appearances of yours.'

'What are you talking about?'

'You suddenly appeared in our box at the theatre!'

'No I didn't. I wasn't anywhere near your theatre.'

'You did!' The Lamb was indignant. 'And you did something mighty funny with the applause.'

'Shh!' Jane hissed. 'Let him explain.'

'Thank you, Jane.' The Psammead was gracious. 'After you'd all gone to the theatre, I felt so very feeble and ill that I wished and wished to die – and then I had a strange dream. I heard a voice that said I could have my health and strength if I gave in and agreed to start my programme of repentance.'

His mouth stretched into a smirk, as if he expected to be thanked.

'Er – good for you,' Edie said quickly. 'But you won't have to go away, will you?'

'No, my dear Edie, it's a correspondence course that I can do from the comfort of my own sand bath.'

'What'll you have to do? Just be sorry?' the Lamb asked.

'Yes, but that sounds too easy,' the Psammead sighed. 'At first, I was stubborn – I don't like thinking of myself as a criminal, and I don't like admitting that any of my past actions were wrong. But if I'm ever to find peace I must face up to one or two little incidents from my days as a desert god, and truly understand the suffering I apparently caused. The moment I gave in, the power poured back into me and I felt – as the Lamb would say – completely top-hole.'

'But why did we see you at the theatre?'

125

'I have no idea. I was in a dark chamber, where my strength poured back in a great roar.'

'I think I sort of understand,' Jane said. 'It was the applause that gave you strength – ordinary applause wouldn't have done anything. Don't you see? Everyone was clapping *because they believed in fairies*! I bet that had something to do with it.'

'So some sort of fairy worship still exists,' the Psammead said. 'Most gratifying! Any time I feel a little out of sorts, I simply need to find a performance of *Peter Pan* and I'll be right as ninepence.'

'But I don't think he's quite grasped the exact meaning of what he's promised,' Jane said, when they left the attic. 'He still doesn't get the first thing about being sorry.'

Eleven

HOSPITAL BLUE

I**N THE EARLY SPRING OF** 1915 they saw Cyril properly, when he came home on leave. He brought a real German bullet for the Lamb and a little glass globe for Edie. Inside was a tiny model of a French village with a church, and when you shook it the globe filled with whirling snowflakes.

The Psammead had never seen a snow globe and thought it was beautiful. 'I only wish I'd owned such a thing in my days as a god! My dear Cyril, where did you find this exquisite treasure?'

'It's not exactly a treasure,' Cyril said. 'I was behind the lines in rest-billets, and I bought it in the local market. An old biddy had a whole tray of them – they're doing a brisk trade in overpriced souvenirs over there. That town must've been a sleepy sort of place before the war. Anyhow, good luck to them. The

French are having a rotten time of it, far worse than us. You should see how the Huns have ripped up their countryside. Harper says he's fighting to stop them doing the same to ours.'

When he talked about the war, which he hardly ever did, Cyril's voice hardened and he seemed to be looking through them all, as if he'd left part of himself behind. Mother said he looked older and thinner, and Mrs Field tried to give him suet pudding at every meal to build him up. They wanted to lay on all sorts of entertainments for him, from theatres to parties, but Cyril was quite happy to spend the entire two weeks either sleeping, going out for long walks on his own, or sitting in the old nursery with his brother and sisters and the Psammead.

Robert was in the middle of exams, but managed to dash home for Cyril's last weekend. Though the children didn't go on about it, being together again was wonderful. Edie thought the White House felt comfortably complete, like a person after a big meal.

On the last day of his leave, which was warm and sunny, Cyril persuaded the Psammead to come out into the garden for a little fresh air. 'I'm sure it's not good for you to be stuffed in the attic all day – you'll go mouldy.'

The Psammead said he would do nothing of the kind, but agreed to the outing because he wanted to be nice on Cyril's last day. The six of them went out directly after lunch, with the Psammead riding cosily inside Cyril's big tweed coat.

Cyril found it easier to talk about the war when they were out in the open. He told them about the truce they'd seen when they visited him on Christmas Day, which had spread for miles along the lines. 'My chaps just did a bit of shouting and singing, but some were out in No Man's Land playing football with the Huns, and giving them Red Cross chocolate. It couldn't last long, of course – or the whole war would have started to look absolutely silly.'

'It is silly,' sniffed the Psammead. 'All those men dying, for the sake of a few yards of mud!'

Cyril smiled. 'Since when have you cared about men dying?'

'I didn't WASTE my own soldiers. I was very thrifty and only killed prisoners.'

'Oh, Psammead, how refreshingly awful you are! We don't kill prisoners these days.'

'You don't? What do you do with them? Good gracious – is this ANOTHER thing I have to repent about?'

'I took some prisoners once,' Cyril said, looking ahead at a line of poplar trees. 'I stumbled on four German officers who didn't realise their trench had been overrun. I don't know which of us was more surprised. I felt far too polite to shoot them – luckily they decided to surrender, and I took them back to our lines for tea. They were rather decent.'

'Decent!' the Psammead sniffed. 'What kind of war do you call this? You're supposed to HATE the Germans.'

'There are too many of them to hate individually,' Cyril said. 'They're only following orders.'

'Is that where you got my bullet?' the Lamb asked. 'Yes, it was in one of the guns I took off them.'

'My hat – wait till I show Winterbum! What happened to your prisoners?'

'I don't know. I expect they're in a camp somewhere. Sometimes I think they're well out of it.'

'My dear Cyril,' the Psammead said, 'I've tried out all sorts of wishes to keep you at home, but none of them worked. It looks as if you'll have to go back.'

Cyril smiled. 'Of course I'm going back! The beastly bits are horribly beastly, but the war's sort of at the centre of reality. It's impossible to be anywhere else.'

'Yes, it's looking that way,' Robert said. 'I won't be able to duck out for much longer.'

They were all quiet.

'Don't rush into anything,' Cyril said. 'You might be too much of a weed to pass the medical.'

Robert was serious. 'You know the government's talking about conscription.' He added, to Edie, 'That's when they force people to join the army if there aren't enough volunteers. I'll join up before they have to force me. I'm already doing army drill three times a week, with what's left of the Officer Training Corps at my college – and you're right, we're a rather wet-looking bunch of remnants. Our ancient sergeant calls us things I can't repeat in front of girls or sand fairies.'

'Back in my days of divinity,' the Psammead began, 'When I ruled the—'

'NO!' the Lamb groaned rudely. 'I don't want to hear another thing about your blood-soaked reign – it's a waste of Squirrel being here. We want to hear about the REAL war.'

'I BEG your pardon?' The Psammead's eyes telescoped back into his furious face.

'Please, please don't be offended!' Edie cried out. 'Don't go into one of your huffs!'

131

'Lamb, you have grown up into a very IMPUDENT boy. I was simply trying to chat with your brother, warrior to warrior.' The Psammead cancelled his huff; he wanted to make the most of Cyril's leave as much as anyone. 'People at home can't imagine what it's like to fight a war. But I understand.'

'I rather doubt that,' Cyril said. 'Wars have changed a bit since your day.'

'Wars never change – they're still basically two sides trying to kill each other.'

'Yes, but your army didn't have modern weapons. One of our machine guns could see off the whole lot of them in about thirty seconds.'

'We shouldn't spoil your leave talking about the war,' Anthea said, taking Cyril's arm.

'I don't mind. There are one or two good things about life at the front – my boys, for instance, the best bunch you ever saw. I'd walk through fire for every single one of them. And I'm looking forward to seeing good old Harper again. We've planned a slap-up dinner at the Criterion before we catch our train.'

★

It was much harder to say goodbye to him this time. Mother put her hands on his shoulders and looked into his face. 'I feel as if you're only half here – as if most of you had already gone back.'

He kissed her. 'Don't fret, Mother – I'm always incredibly careful.'

The house was as flat as a burst balloon when he'd gone, and worse when Robert went back to Cambridge the next day.

Father shook Robert's hand. 'Don't make up your mind about the army until you've talked to me.'

'They won't be interested in Bobs,' Mother said; she refused to believe it was possible that anyone would expect to take away another of her sons. 'Not with his eyesight, and he's never been strong.'

'Anyway, it can't go on much longer,' Father said. 'The spring offensive should sort things out.'

This was the sort of thing people were saying now when they wanted to sound cheery, but even Edie had stopped believing it. Whatever an 'offensive' was, more and more men were dying; the newspapers ran long lists of the dead and wounded. In Edie's class at Poplar House, Agnes the bully had lost her youngest uncle, and kind Miss Poole her brother. So many people wore black clothes and armbands wherever you looked.

'I was so sorry for Agnes that I gave her one of my toffees,' Edie told the Psammead during their afternoon session in the attic. 'Poor thing, her eyes were swollen up like golf balls from crying. Miss Poole hasn't come back yet, because she has to take care of her mother. There are so many sad people nowadays that sadness looks normal.'

'Careful!' The Psammead sank deeper into the sand. 'Not thinking of crying yourself, I hope.'

'Oh, stow it – I'm not crying.' Edie was less perfectly polite to him these days. 'What about your own tears, anyway – do they hurt too?'

'Psammeads don't cry.'

'You mean, you've never cried?'

'I don't have any tears of my own.'

'Well, you'll just have to put up with the teary atmosphere,' Edie said, more sharply than usual; much as she loved the Psammead, she sometimes thought his hearts were as hard as two little walnuts. 'Nobody can help crying when they're by themselves. I know Anthea cries. And not just because she's worried about Cyril.'

'Really?' The Psammead emerged again; he was nosey and fond of gossip, especially now that he'd got his strength back. 'Why does Anthea cry?'

'She's worried about Ernie,' Edie said. 'I'm pretty worried about him too. Our professor hasn't heard from him for weeks and weeks.'

★

'Oh!' Anthea cried out. In a flash, the expression on her face turned from sadness to joy.

'What it is, dear?' Mother asked. 'Who is that letter from?'

'Nobody, I mean Jimmy – the Professor.'

'Ah,' Mother said, and went on spreading marmalade on her toast, though she didn't look quite satisfied.

The family were all sitting around the table having breakfast. Anthea raised her eyebrows meaningfully at her siblings. 'He's heard from Mr Haywood.'

'Good stuff!' the Lamb said. 'Is he all right?'

'He was badly wounded at Ypres – he's lost one of his legs.' Her voice wobbled dangerously and she paused to swallow hard. 'But he's alive, and good old Jimmy says he's going to be all right.'

'Poor thing!' Edie hated to think of the nimble Ernie hobbling on one foot.

'He's just been moved to the Endell Street Military Hospital in Covent Garden. He sent a postcard to Jimmy because he doesn't have anyone else. He must be so lonely.'

'That's the hospital where all the doctors are women,' Jane said. 'So you see, women doctors absolutely do exist.'

'Jane, must we start all this again?' Mother sighed.

'I'm simply pointing it out.' Jane had said it to distract Mother from looking too closely at Anthea, who had tears on her eyelashes, and it had worked.

'Well, I don't want to hear any more about it, thank you – and nobody's going to welcome a doctor with those inky fingers.'

'Bobs pinched the pumice stone and I can't rub it off with just soap.'

Anthea had quickly wiped her eyes. 'I think we ought to visit him.'

'Rather,' the Lamb said. 'Losing a leg is one of the beastliest things I can think of, next to going blind. Or losing both legs. Or losing both arms.'

'Darling, don't be morbid,' Mother murmured.

'Jimmy wants us to take Mr Haywood some books,' Anthea said. 'We can drop in at Old Nurse's on the way and pick them up, as it's near the hospital.'

'If Jimmy's sending them, I bet they're extremely boring books,' Jane said, smiling. 'And not what any normal wounded soldier would want to read when they're ill. I vote we dig up a couple of nice, amusing ones, and we know Mr Haywood likes the *New Citizen*.'

Father, hidden behind a wall of newspaper, heard the name of his magazine. 'Good for him – he can have a copy of the latest edition, with my compliments.'

'Anthea,' Mother said, 'do I know anything about this young man?'

Nobody had said anything to Edie, but she knew perfectly well that Mother had noticed the blushy way Anthea behaved whenever anyone mentioned Ernie. She'd heard the big girls whispering about it, and knew that Jane was doing her best to damp down Mother's suspicions.

'We've told you about him,' Jane said. 'He's a friend of the Professor's, and a sort of assistant. He knows a lot about ancient history.'

'He's extremely nice,' Edie said. 'Old Nurse says he has a very taking way with him.'

Mother looked at Anthea. 'And he's serving in the army?'

'Yes,' Anthea said.

'He's an officer, of course.'

'No.'

'I beg your pardon?' Mother's hand, holding toast, froze in mid-air.

'He's a private,' the Lamb said. 'But when he's well enough, he's going to work as the Professor's secretary. I'm sure he can still do that with one leg.'

'I see.' Mother's voice was faint with doubt.

'Poor young chap.' Father lowered his newspaper. 'Of course you must visit him.' He added, to Mother, 'No harm in it if they all go. Errand of mercy, and all that.'

'I suppose not – if they're simply going to cheer him up.'

And it was settled. Anthea, blazing with energy, fired off postcards to Jimmy and Old Nurse to say they would be there for lunch on Saturday.

'And I've had a wonderful idea,' she told the others when they were upstairs without the parents. 'Let's take the Psammead.'

'Hmm,' the Lamb said. 'He was a bit of a nuisance last time. I'd rather leave him out of it.'

'No, let's take him,' Jane said. Mr Haywood likes him, and it'll be a good chance to try out his new carrier.' Jane had a flair for engineering – she was the best in the family at mending bicycles – and she had made a new Psammead-carrier out of a string shopping bag and a leather belt, which was far sturdier than the old one. It was decided that she should carry him this time – under her coat, which had a cape over the shoulders to hide the strange lump under her left arm.

'Most comfortable,' the Psammead said approvingly. 'Quite a miracle of construction. I may even get a wink of sleep, if you don't bounce me about too much.'

★

On Saturday morning they packed the big basket with gifts for Ernie – books, magazines and a box of very good shortbread made by Anthea. The Lamb put in one of his favourite adventure stories, and Edie had spent two weeks' pocket money on a bag of barley-sugar twists (Mrs Trent, who ran at the village shop and post office, had put in extra when she heard they were for a wounded soldier).

At Old Nurse's house, Jimmy had been waiting for them impatiently. 'Now, how much can you carry? I'd like Haywood to see all three volumes of this – and these photographs from the museum at Stuttgart—'

'Steady on,' the Lamb said, 'we haven't got a wheelbarrow.'

Jimmy wanted them to take Ernie an enormous pile of heavy books, but Anthea talked him down to three.

'But these are vital for the research into my next paper – the paper that will make my reputation! And those female dragons at the hospital won't let me see him, though I explained that I was bringing him important work. They think I'm some kind of slave-driver.' He smiled dreamily at the Psammead, perched on his desk. 'Like you.'

'I know I'm a fascinating subject,' the Psammead said, 'but I'm not sure I like you raking up the past. Frankly, there are certain incidents I'd rather forget.'

'Certain crimes, you mean,' the Lamb said, grinning.

The Psammead's whiskers bristled irritably. 'It's a respectable history paper – not a police report. This scholar and his warrior will only tell of my GLORY.'

'You're a key to the hidden history of the ancient

world,' the Professor said. 'Now that I know about you, all kind of texts suddenly become clear. I've been taking a new look at the sad story of the young lovers Osman and Tulap.'

'It's all a pack of LIES!' the Psammead snapped. 'Young lovers PHOOEY! They were nothing but a pair of troublemakers!' He pulled in his eyes as far as they would go and folded up his long arms and legs until he was a compact furry ball of deep sulking.

'Oh dear, I didn't mean to annoy him.' Jimmy looked at them all properly, as if waking from a trance. 'Please send poor Haywood my best wishes. Tell him he must get well as fast as possible – he's the only person who can be trusted to help me with my work.'

★

'But I can't think why Ernie would want to read books like these,' the Lamb said when they were walking along Bloomsbury Street towards Covent Garden. 'Even the footnotes have got footnotes.'

The Military Hospital took up one side of the narrow street; it was a grim, sooty building that had once been a workhouse. The four children and the hidden sand fairy walked into a large, tiled hallway that smelled of disinfectant and boiled cabbage. Through an open door they could see a sitting room with armchairs and small tables, where soldiers in blue uniforms smoked and read newspapers. The man nearest to them had an empty sleeve pinned across his chest.

'Hospital blue,' Anthea said, 'the uniform of the wounded.' Her voice wobbled and she was very nervous.

A nurse with grey hair came briskly across the hall. 'May I help you?'

'We'd like to see Private Haywood, please,' Anthea said. 'I understand this is visiting hour.'

The nurse looked at them doubtfully. 'Just a moment,' she said and hurried away.

'Crikey, wouldn't I love a guided tour of this place!' Jane muttered.

A thin lady in a white coat – with smooth dark hair and a face like a stern wooden doll – came into the hall.

'I am Dr Garrett Anderson,' she said. 'I understand you've come to see Private Haywood.'

'Yes,' Edie said. 'We've brought him some books and things.'

'May I know who you are? We don't generally allow children in, and I'm not sure he's well enough for a host of visitors.'

This was a terrible let-down.

'Ernie – Private Haywood – doesn't have a family,' the Lamb said boldly. 'We're the nearest thing, and I promise he'll be no end pleased to see us. We won't stay too long and we won't make a row.'

The doctor was still stern, but there was a glint of a smile at the corners of her mouth. 'I'll hold you to that, young man. The patients here are all recovering from serious wounds and mustn't be disturbed or upset.'

'We'll be as quiet as mice,' the Lamb assured her. 'Honour bright!'

'Hmmm, he could certainly do with a bit of cheering up – the poor boy hasn't had a single visitor, unless you count one rather dotty gentleman who wanted him to do some sort of work.' (They all recognised Jimmy from this description.) 'Very well, I'll allow you ten minutes. Follow me, please.'

She led them through a door covered with green felt and along a short corridor into a bare, bright conservatory that had been converted into a hospital room. Beside the metal-framed bed was a wheelchair with a thin, sagging figure sitting in it. Edie was about to say this wasn't Ernie, but the doctor said, 'Here are some visitors for you, Private Haywood.'

'Visitors?' Ernie raised his head, and when he saw them Edie suddenly understood what the books meant when they said a person's face 'lit up'; it was like seeing the sun rise behind his eyes. 'You!'

'Don't let him get too excited – this is only his first day out of bed.' The doctor left the room.

The moment the door shut behind her, Anthea let out a little cry and ran to Ernie. She dropped to her knees in front of him, and they clasped each other's hands as if they would never let go.

'You!' Ernie said again. He smiled dazedly at the rest of them. 'All of you – this is a bit of all right!'

'I'm sorry about your leg,' said a muffled voice under Jane's coat. 'If I still had my full powers I'd wish you a new one – at least till sunset.'

Ernie burst out laughing. 'I don't believe it – you've brought his nibs!'

Twelve

YOUNG LOVERS

JANE UNWRAPPED THE PSAMMEAD from his new carrier, and the sight of his small, brown body sitting on the smooth white bed put an end to any awkwardness. Ernie was so pleased to see them that he looked younger and stronger by the minute, and more like his real self. He was delighted with the shortbread and Edie's barley-sugar twists, and the Lamb's adventure story, one of a popular sixpenny series about a hero named Captain Dick Doughty. 'Good-oh – I like these, and I haven't read this one yet.'

'I knew you'd like it,' the Lamb said. 'Anthea thinks it's lurid, but you can't spend all your time reading the Professor's dull old tomes.'

'Not dull to me. I can't wait to get a look at them. They have a decent enough library here, but I went

145

through it all in about a week, and now I'm so bored I'm losing my mind.' Ernie's left leg had been cut off just below the knee; his blue trouser-leg was neatly pinned over the stump. They all tried not to stare at it. 'How is the old Prof, anyway?'

'Very well,' the Psammead said. 'I permitted him to worship me for a few minutes this morning – his new paper is all about me.'

'That's right, chum,' Ernie said. 'You've turned his head. Since he met you, he hasn't thought about anything else.'

'Very understandable.' The vain sand fairy was plump with pride. 'Now, do tell us how your leg got blown off.'

'Psammead!' the Lamb hissed.

'Did you keep it and bring it home?'

Ernie laughed. 'It got left behind, somewhere along the Menin Road, in the Ypres Salient. I don't think I'll bother to go back for it.'

'I'm so sorry,' Anthea said, her whole heart in her voice. 'You've had a dreadful time.'

'It could've been worse.'

'Indeed it could,' the Psammead said. 'It might have been your head.'

'Stop it,' Jane said. 'We're meant to be cheering him up!'

'My dear Jane, I'm looking on the bright side – this warrior's wound is a splendid piece of luck. It means he won't have to go back to the war, so he'll be free to help the Professor with the great book he's writing about ME.'

'You call that LUCK?' The Lamb was indignant. 'That old skeleton-priestess woman was right – you're heartless, and you only think about yourself. If this is your idea of repenting—'

'Well, he's right in a way,' Ernie said, grinning. 'When I get out of here I'll be able to read and write as much as I like, and I can hardly wait to get started. Before I was wounded the Prof was sending me long letters about all the new discoveries he's made.'

'Hmmm,' the Psammead said. 'About me?'

'You and your distinguished career.'

'Yes, it was very distinguished. But he mentioned something this morning that you needn't bother to look into. The old story of Osman and Tulap is just that – an old story.' The Psammead looked incredibly shifty. 'Tell him not to waste his time.'

'He said they were young lovers,' Edie remembered.

147

'And you said they were troublemakers.'

'Troublemakers, eh?' Ernie gazed at the Psammead. 'So they weren't just a story.'

The Psammead's whiskers shivered. 'All these ancient legends have some basis in fact.'

'It's a tragic tale – blimey, I can hardly believe I'm talking to the desert god himself! This isn't a dream, is it?'

'No, you're not dreaming.' Anthea squeezed Ernie's hand. 'Who were they?'

'Tulap was a beautiful maiden in the temple of the high priestess – the temple maidens were very posh girls, like princesses. And Osman was a runaway slave from the kingdom of a certain desert tyrant.'

'Let me guess,' Jane said, 'a sand fairy.'

'If he hadn't run away I would've thrown him out!' snapped the Psammead. 'He organised a rebellion and took two hundred of my best slaves with him!'

'He escaped to Akkad,' Ernie went on. 'And he fell in love with Tulap. The high priestess gave her blessing and they got married. But just as they were running into each other's arms, the angry desert god turned them both into pillars of stone. There they stand to this day, arms eternally outstretched, in the middle of the

148

Akkadian desert. The legend says that when the stars are at their brightest, they can be heard singing love songs to each other.'

'Oh, how gloriously romantic!' Anthea sighed.

'Kindly don't get SOPPY,' the Psammead said.

'Why did you have to turn those poor young lovers to stone?' Jane asked. 'It was beastly of you!'

'I wanted them to be a warning to anyone else who felt like disobeying me,' the Psammead mumbled furiously. 'He ran away with all my keys! It was very inconvenient.'

'I can't imagine how the Prof's going to put all this in a book,' Ernie said. 'Nobody will believe a word of it.'

Edie stroked the Psammead's guilty little head. 'You were very mean in the past, but I'm sure you're sorry now.'

'He's never sorry,' the Lamb said darkly. 'Stop making excuses for him.'

'Of course I'm sorry!' spat the Psammead. 'There – satisfied? I had no idea it would all be raked up again thousands of years later!'

'In other words,' the Lamb said, 'you're just sorry you got found out!'

'Pooh!' The Psammead rolled himself into a tight

ball of defiance, which made them all burst out laughing.

And then the door handle rattled, and there was only just time to shove the angry sand fairy back in his carrier before the doctor swept into the room.

'Private Haywood, what is going on in here? I could hear you all from the bottom of the corridor!'

'Beg your pardon, Doctor,' Ernie said. 'We had a bit of catching up to do.'

'I daresay – but visiting hour is over for today.'

She stood, stern and stiff and staring narrowly at Jane's coat while they said their goodbyes to Ernie, then she marched them back to the front door as if escorting criminals.

On the doorstep, however, she suddenly softened. 'I know exactly what you're doing,' she told Jane. 'I saw you hiding it under your coat.'

'Whh-what?' Jane turned bright red.

'Look here,' the doctor said, lowering her voice, 'you're not the first to smuggle in someone's pet dog, and you probably won't be the last – but it's completely against hospital rules, and you mustn't do it again.'

She had glimpsed the Psammead but thought he was a dog, which was a great relief.

'We won't,' Jane said quickly. 'Sorry.'

'I'm not going to tell you off this time, because your dog has cheered my patient up no end.'

'Thank you, Doctor,' they all said.

'And we're sorry about the noise,' the Lamb added.

The doctor smiled. 'I won't tell you off about that either. I happen to think laughter is rather a nice noise, as noises go.'

★

'It was all I could do not to shout at her,' the Psammead said. 'A dog, indeed! Such gormless creatures.'

'Do stop going on about it.' The Lamb lay on his back, chewing a thick piece of liquorice. 'I'm jolly glad you didn't shout at Doctor Garrett Anderson – she turned out to be an A1 brick. And you're spoiling the first halfway decent day we've had all year.'

'Her mother was very famous,' said Jane. 'She was the first woman in Britain to qualify as a physician.'

It was a Saturday afternoon, a month after their visit to Ernie, and so warm and sunny that the Lamb and Edie had taken the Psammead on an outing to the gravel pit at the bottom of the garden. He sat

151

in a comfortable hollow, basking in the summery heat.

'Yes, it's very pleasant to feel the warm air on my fur, and it reminds me of a lovely dream I had last night, about a green field all covered with white flowers. I wonder if that peaceful place – wherever it is – could be the place where I'm going?'

'I hope you never leave.' Edie's lap was filled with daisies, as she was trying to make a daisy chain for the Psammead. 'It's so lovely having you here – I can hardly bear to think of life without you.'

'But he'll have to leave eventually, however long his repentance takes,' the Lamb said. 'He can't carry on living in the attic after we're all dead.'

'Why not? I've already thought about this. When we're all dead, our children can take over looking after him. We can leave him in our wills.'

'Excuse me,' the Psammead said huffily, 'I'm not a clock or a vase – or a family pet.'

The Lamb sat up. 'That's exactly your trouble, Edie – you treat him like a pet.'

'I do not!'

'You brush his fur and stroke him and try to knit him tiny scarves, forgetting he was once a tyrannical desert god with the power to turn lovers into stone.'

'Please,' the Psammead said, pursing his mouth, 'stop going on about that wretched couple!'

'Osman and Tulap,' Edie said; she'd been very moved by the story of the tragic lovers. 'Why were you so mean to them?'

'Runaway slaves can't go round falling in love with temple maidens, and that's that!'

'I don't see why not,' the Lamb said.

'It's completely unsuitable, that's why – Tulap was high-born and Osman was common.'

'That doesn't matter,' Edie said. 'You can't tell people not to fall in love. I know we've argued about this a lot, but I still say you were cruel to them.'

'And I keep telling you – everyone was cruel in those days.'

'They only wanted to be together.'

'Well, they're together now, aren't they? Albeit as rather crumbly pillars of stone.' The Psammead's eyes zoomed round to the Lamb. 'What are you laughing at?'

'You,' the Lamb said, 'because you're so frightful. Squirrel says you've got an armour-plated conscience.'

Edie sighed romantically. 'Oh, I w—'

'Careful!' cried the Psammead. 'I can't control random wishes!'

'—WISH I could see those lovers!'

The earth fell away underneath them. Edie shrieked and made a grab at the Psammead.

'Edie, you CLOT!' yelled the Lamb. He braced himself for the heat and flies of the Psammead's desert home, thousands of years in the past.

When the wind died down, however, there was no desert heat. The sheer ordinariness of the place they had come to hit them like a slap. Wherever they were, it looked nothing at all like an ancient civilisation, and everything like a park in modern London.

They were on the top of a grassy hill with a fine view of the city. Below them they could see a bandstand and a bowling green. There were nannies pushing prams, little children feeding ducks beside the pond, and couples strolling arm in arm.

'This is nice.' Edie was very relieved to see that her impulsive wish hadn't carried them off to anywhere too strange.

'I've been here before,' the Lamb said. 'When I was

154

a baby and we lived in Camden Town. I'm pretty sure this is Hampstead Heath.'

'Wherever it is,' the Psammead said, 'it's an awful lot nicer than those dangerous ancient days. Let's be grateful for small mercies.'

Someone was coming up the steep path on their left – a soldier in a blue uniform, making a great effort to move quickly on a pair of crutches.

'Ernie!' the Lamb and Edie cried together.

Ernie was red-faced and breathless; they heard him gasping as he swung past them.

'Ernie – wait for me!' a voice called from the bottom of the path.

It was Anthea, also out of breath, pushing an empty wheelchair.

'Ah – the lovers,' the Psammead said. 'Your wish has been granted.'

'What – Ernie and Panther?' the Lamb was disgusted. 'They're not lovers!'

Unlike the Lamb, Edie didn't think the word 'lover' was an insult. 'Gosh, how romantic!'

The Lamb made being-sick noises.

'Shut up. We know Ernie thinks Anthea's pretty – so why shouldn't they fall in love?'

'Of course these two are in love,' the Psammead said. 'These are the lovers the universe has chosen to show me.'

'But they're nothing like Osman and Tulap,' Edie said, watching Anthea as she puffed up the steep path with the wheelchair. 'Nobody's going to turn them to stone. This is the modern world, and things like that don't happen.'

'I'll just ask you one question,' the Psammead said. 'What would your mother say if she were here?'

'She'd be – pleased.' Edie was suddenly doubtful, remembering how stiff and odd their mother had been when they told her about the hospital visit.

'I don't know about that,' the Lamb said. 'If this is still the same Saturday, I heard Anthea telling Mother she was going sketching this afternoon, with two girls from her old art class.'

The two children were silent; there was something horribly uncomfortable about knowing that Anthea had lied to Mother so coolly.

Edie and the Lamb were standing near a wooden bench, where Ernie collapsed with a groan. 'Made it!'

Anthea caught up with him and collapsed beside him. They both laughed breathlessly.

156

'You only had to do a few yards,' she said. 'You didn't have to go at it full-tilt.'

'I go at everything full-tilt,' Ernie said. 'As I daresay you've noticed.'

'Look here, Psammead,' the Lamb said, 'we shouldn't be eavesdropping – this makes me feel like the lowest kind of sneak.'

'Me too,' Edie said. 'Can you take us home now?'

'No, we'll just have to wait it out.'

'Then we mustn't listen to them. Let's walk away.'

'Stop!' yelped the Psammead. 'You can't disobey – and neither can I. Don't you see?'

The Lamb and Edie – with Edie clutching the Psammead tightly – began to walk down the hill. But somehow, without turning around, they suddenly found they were walking up the hill again. Wherever they went, all paths led back to Anthea and Ernie.

'You see?' the Psammead settled more comfortably in Edie's arms. 'Now listen quietly.'

'It's a good place, that hospital,' Ernie was saying. 'I've fallen on my feet all right.' A grin flashed across his face. 'My foot, I mean. The food's the best I've ever had in my life. But I'm itching to get back into the world. The doctor reckons I'm doing really well.'

He was as handsome as ever, Edie decided, now that his face had lost that hungry, scraped-out look she'd seen in the hospital – and he was still worthy of being her crackation.

'When will you be ready for your false leg?' Anthea asked.

'I'm ready now, but there's a national shortage of left feet, so I'll have to wait.'

'I'm glad about one thing – I'm glad you won't have to go back to the war. What will you do?'

'Professor Knight offered me a job as his assistant,' Ernie said. 'He can't afford to pay much, but I'll get my room and board at Mrs Taylor's – and all the ancient history I can eat.'

'And we'll be able to see each other more often,' Anthea said softly, clasping Ernie's hand.

'No.' He shook his head. 'We won't. We can't go on seeing each other. It's got to stop.'

'But – why?'

'Come on, you know why,' Ernie said. 'This isn't right. I shouldn't have let myself fall for you so deeply. That's why I sent the postcard to the Prof and not to you. I want to marry you, but you know it's hopeless – and that means it's not right to carry on as lovers.'

'I don't care. I nearly lost you,' Anthea said, 'and I'm not letting you go ever again.'

The Lamb groaned with embarrassment; the Psammead hissed, 'Shhh!'

'You're a high-born temple maiden,' Ernie said, 'and I'm just a runaway slave.'

'Don't joke about it!'

'I'm not joking. Your people are gentlefolk and you're a lady. I'm a docker's son, with no education, one leg, an East End accent that could strip paint – and I only joined the army because I was hungry. You'd be surprised how many of us took the King's shilling to get three meals a day. I'm as common as it gets, and it's no good you saying you don't care. Your parents would care, all right. Your dad's all for socialism and the rights of the working man, but if he could see us now, he'd punch my lights out. That's the way the world is.'

They sat in silence, hands clasped, gazing out at the view of the city.

'I hate the world sometimes,' Anthea said. 'The unfairness of it. I won't force you to see me if you don't want to – but nobody can stop me loving you, and I'll wait for you all my life if I have to.'

Ernie gently raised her hand to his lips.

And then the world turned a somersault, and the Lamb, Edie and the Psammead were back in the gravel pit.

★

'Phew!' the Lamb gasped. 'Thank goodness – I was afraid we'd have to watch them kissing.'

'Poor Panther,' Edie said. 'And poor Ernie – I don't know about Father but would Mother really be so against them, if she found out?'

The Lamb thought about this. 'She wouldn't be all that keen.'

'But why? Ernie's so nice.'

'You know how she goes on about "our sort of people". She wouldn't think he was our sort, that's all.'

'I still don't see why that's so dreadful.' Edie had decided that the love affair was romantic and beautiful. 'I think it would be ripping if they got married – I'd love to be a bridesmaid.'

'I'm utterly drained,' the Psammead said. 'But I think I get the point. If time could be turned back, I might not punish Osman and Tulap so severely. It's a shame to keep young lovers apart.'

Thirteen

THE LOWEST OF
THE LOW

Aᴺᵀᴴᴱᴬ ᵂᴬˢ ᴹᴼᴿᵀᴵᶠᴵᴱᴰ ᵂᴴᴱᴺ they told her what they'd seen. She covered her burning face with her hands.

'Honestly, we didn't listen on purpose,' Edie said. 'We tried to walk away – but then the world sort of swung round and we were walking towards you again.'

'It wasn't our fault,' the Lamb said. 'Edie wanted to see those ancient lovers, but we got you and Ernie instead. Sorry.'

'Oh, I'm not cross with you,' Anthea said, uncovering her face reluctantly. 'I'm just so dreadfully embarrassed that you heard me telling all those whoppers about going sketching. I hate lying.'

'And you're very bad at it,' Jane said. 'You turn

bright red and your voice goes squeaky. I'm rather amazed the parents didn't notice.'

It was Saturday evening, after dinner, and the parents had gone over to Windytops to play bridge with the Winterbottoms. The children had the sitting room to themselves and Edie had tried to persuade the Psammead to come downstairs, but the afternoon's adventure had made him snappish and he was asleep in his sand bath.

'Don't!' Anthea groaned. 'I'll never live this down – that troublesome Psammead! Thanks to him I've been caught canoodling in the park with a soldier, like a naughty parlourmaid.'

'Steady on,' Jane murmured.

'Well, that's how it looks.'

'You should've told us,' Edie said. 'It's mean that you only told Jane. I suppose that's what you've been whispering about. Actually, I knew perfectly well that something was going on.'

'The babes know everything now,' Jane said. 'You might as well come clean. You told Bobs and Cyril.'

'Look, if you're going to talk about frightful things like LOVE, I'm leaving,' the Lamb said. 'I'm glad you didn't tell us.'

Anthea smiled for the first time. 'I'll make it as unsoppy as I can. As you've probably guessed, the sordid fact is that I've been carrying on with Ernie in secret. The week after we first met, I ran into him again while I was Christmas shopping in Oxford Street – completely accidentally. After that, we knew we had to meet again. By the time we realised we were in love, it was too late to do anything about it. Ernie tried to put me off before he went to France, but it was no use.'

Edie took Anthea's hand. 'What'll you do now?'

'Ernie won't allow me to say we're engaged, when the whole thing is so impossible. He says it's pointless even to think about it until he's found a way of earning a living. But I'm afraid I'm bound to upset Mother anyway.' She looked at her youngest brother and sister. 'I needed to get away and do something proper – it's silly to waste time painting and paying calls when this war is so terrible. I've signed up to be a VAD.'

They knew this stood for 'Voluntary Aid Detachment'; the hospitals were swamped with casualties, and there was a desperate shortage of regular trained nurses. The VADs were partly trained volunteers, like Anthea.

'It's perfectly splendid of you,' Jane said. 'I do wish I could go with you – it's infuriating that they won't take seventeen-year-olds, which is what I'll be in a couple of weeks.'

'You're leaving?' This was the headline for Edie, who couldn't imagine the White House – or the world – without Anthea. She had always been there, as constant as Mother and Father, or the moon and the sun.

'Darling,' Anthea said, 'it won't be for long.'

'But you'll have to see such awful things – bones and blood—'

'That's another reason they should take me,' Jane said. 'I'm not in the least bothered by the sight of blood. And it would be such a splendid way to start my training as a doctor.'

Since the visit to Ernie's military hospital, and their meeting with Dr Garrett Anderson, Jane was even more determined to become a doctor. One of the teachers at school had told her about the London School of Medicine for Women, which was attached to the University of London, but her parents hated the idea; Mother thought studying medicine would ruin Jane's chances of getting married, while Father said it was too expensive, 'and probably chock-full of whiskered old suffragettes.'

'But why do you have to go away now?' Edie asked. 'Just when Ernie's come back?' She didn't quite understand why the lovers couldn't see each other.

'They need every pair of hands,' Anthea said. 'And I'm not going to spend my days pining for Ernie like some swooning maiden. I'm not sure how I'll feel about gruesome sights, but I'm sure I can get used to it – I just know I have to do something for this war, because it swallows up everything else.'

'We'll miss you horribly,' Jane said.

'I'll miss all of you – but at least you'll be free to visit Old Nurse's house. Ernie says I mustn't visit while he's there, but he'll be delighted to see you lot and the Psammead.'

'And we can write to you,' Jane said, 'to tell you how he's getting on.'

'Exactly,' Anthea said. 'You don't have to spy on him, just tell me he's all right.'

'When do you have to go?' Like Edie, the Lamb was trying, and failing, to imagine the White House without Anthea.

'I heard this morning,' she said. 'I start in a month,

as a probationer at St George's Hospital in Hyde Park Corner. I haven't told Mother yet, but I didn't see the point of having a row about it until I knew I'd definitely been accepted.'

'What's a probationer?' Edie asked.

Anthea laughed softly. 'I asked the same question, and the lady who was interviewing me said, "My dear, you will very soon learn that 'probationer' means 'lowest of the low'."'

Letter from Nurse A. Pemberton,
The Nurses' Home,
St George's Hospital, London W

Dear Jane, Lamb, Edie and Psammead,

Don't read any of this to the parents; the whole truth would only worry them.

How am I? Well, I've reached the end of my first week without dropping dead. St George's is a vast, sprawling red-brick place. I live in the nurses' home in the grounds, in a small and spartan bedroom which I share with a very nice girl called Olive Bloss, whose father is a dentist in

166

*Ripon. It's the first time away from home for both of us,
and somehow that makes the homesickness less agonising.*

*I'm writing in a corner of our common room, where
there is a gas fire and a gramophone and we can make
cocoa. I'm more tired than I've ever been in my entire
life and my hands are so red and raw that I can barely
hold my pen. Don't tell Mother, because she won't like
it, but I spent most of this week scrubbing floors while
being snapped at by a rather beastly sister; she's a
regular trained nurse and she thinks us VADs are just
silly little lady amateurs – I'm sure she saves all the most
disgusting jobs for us. That interviewer spoke truthfully –
in this hospital we certainly are the lowest of the low.*

*One or two of the regular nurses seem quite friendly but
most are horrid to us as a matter of principle. There was
Mother fretting about me with all those young soldiers, but
I haven't seen any soldiers yet – my first patients are some
very sweet old ladies.*

*Please keep reminding Mother about the food. I didn't
tell her the half of it – I'm STARVING all the time!!!
I MUST HAVE FRUITCAKE! (In an airtight tin.)
Chocolate would be lovely and a little jar of salmon paste to
liven up the measly triangles of bread and butter they give*

*us for tea. Olive says her people are sending damson jam
and cinder toffee – just writing about all this heavenly grub
makes my mouth water.*

*How is the P's repentance progressing? Have there been
more sudden appearances? I send you a kiss, dear old furry
rascal, along with hugs and kisses for all of you (Ernie says
I can't send him anything, but I send him a kiss regardless
– Edie, you can give it to him when you see him).*

Your loving

Smallest cog in vast machine,

'Lowest of the Low'

Panther

★

The front door of Old Nurse's house stood open; a
man was putting boxes into a motor van at the kerb.
The hall was crowded with more boxes and piles of
books – and an untidy heap of bones that Jane, the
Lamb and Edie recognised as Maud the skeleton.

'Funny, she's not frightening when she's jumbled
up like that,' Edie said.

168

Old Nurse and Ivy were dabbing their eyes as they watched the boxes and bones being taken away. They were Mr Muldoon's things – the young medical student had been killed in France, when the casualty clearing station where he was working was hit by a shell.

'Such a nice young man, and so brave,' Old Nurse said. 'He was right in the front line, taking care of the wounded without a thought for his own safety. I shan't know my second-floor landing without that blooming skeleton.'

Jane, Edie and the Lamb were very sorry, and their sorrow had a sharp edge of anxiety for Cyril, as all this sort of news did.

The three of them had come to London because the Professor had requested another meeting with the Psammead. They heard Jimmy's agitated voice while they were climbing upstairs.

'The facts are all laid out clear as day, and I don't see why it can't be published exactly as it is! Once you read the symbol correctly the entire legend falls into place. It's not mere speculation – we have it from the mouth of the god himself!'

'But the way you've written it down makes you

sound barmy!' Ernie's voice seemed tired. 'No respectable institution is going to believe you heard it from a sand fairy.'

In the Professor's room they found Ernie at the desk, bent over his notebook. Jimmy was on the hearthrug, in front of the ashy grate, fretfully rubbing his grey hair.

'Kindly let me out, Jane,' the Psammead said from inside Jane's coat. 'It's too warm in here, even by my standards.'

'This coat isn't meant for summer.' Jane took the Psammead out of his carrier and shrugged off her coat with a gasp of relief; it was a dull and rather damp day but she was boiling.

'Well, look who it is.' Ernie's face brightened and he threw down his pencil. 'The perfect excuse to stop for a cup of tea.'

'Good afternoon, warrior,' the Psammead said graciously.

'Good afternoon, your worship.'

'I see that your leg has grown back.'

'Not quite, chum – this is my new false leg,' Ernie said. 'I'm slowly getting used to it, and it's good to have two feet again.'

They all looked down at his feet; the false one wore a very stiff black shoe.

'Does it hurt?' Edie asked.

'Not worth mentioning.'

'When I write to Anthea, can I say about your new leg?'

'Course you can, it's hardly a state secret. Tell her I'm walking without a stick.'

'My dears!' Jimmy finally pulled them into focus. 'No Anthea? But of course, she's gone away too. Only three children today.'

Ernie set the blackened kettle on the gas ring. He gave the Psammead's little head a pat. 'You've turned up at the ideal moment – we were just talking about another story from your shady past. There's a symbol in early Akkadian for "beast of burden", and it can mean either a slave or a donkey. This particular story just about makes sense if you read the word as "slave", but the Prof wants to use the word "donkey" – and that makes the whole thing look absolutely cockeyed!'

'Donkey?' The Psammead's whiskers bristled. 'I don't know any donkeys.'

'Then kindly set us right, O Wise One!' Jimmy

bowed his head. 'Tell us the true story of NIRPIL THE NEWSGIVER.'

'No – because whatever the legend says is a LIE. I call him NIRPIL THE BETRAYER!'

The Lamb chortled unkindly. 'Looks like another crime's catching up with you!'

'I will tell the version that appears on the stone at Stuttgart,' Jimmy said. 'Nirpil was a handsome young prince of a desert tribe, and in his youth he "hung out", as the saying goes, with a certain minor desert god.'

'Minor!' snapped the Psammead. 'How dare you? My power was absolute!'

'Nirpil grew older and wiser,' Jimmy went on, 'and took notice of the desert god's wicked behaviour. Nirpil was the person who reported him to the high priestess, whereupon the angry desert god said, "You supped with kings, now you shall be the lowest of the low," and turned him into a donkey.'

Everyone looked at the Psammead, sulkily hunched on the desk.

'That was horrid of you,' Edie said sadly. 'But I'm getting used to your wicked past.'

'To cut a long story short, the desert god was

deposed by his own people, and that's why he lost most of his powers – everyone stopped worshipping him, and that's all it takes. The high priestess wanted to put him in prison for his many crimes, so he went into hiding in a deep cave and ordered the donkey Nirpil to bring him news and supplies. Unknown to him, however, the donkey had kept all his human intelligence. Every day, using his nose or his hooves, he was painstakingly spelling out a message on a flat hillside, in dozens of small stones – HE'S OVER THERE, with an arrow pointing to the Psammead's cave.'

This was met with silence.

'Well?' the Lamb asked. 'Aren't you going to defend yourself?'

'Pooh! Why should I? Nirpil was a TELLTALE and a SNEAK! It was none of his business what I did with my own slaves!'

'Never mind the rights and wrongs of the case,' Jimmy said. 'Was Nirpil truly a donkey? It'll make all the difference to our book.'

Another silence.

'Yes,' the Psammead finally said, in a small, tight voice.

'There you are, Haywood – I knew it!' Jimmy's face was alight with excitement. 'An actual donkey, with hooves and a tail!'

'Blimey,' Ernie said. 'This puts a new slant on chapter five!' He was chuckling. 'Just don't blame me if they lock both of us in a loony bin when you publish it.'

'Did Nirpil ever get changed back into a human?' Edie asked the Psammead.

'Yes, of course. The spell wore off after a couple of months, though he always had the ears. There's no need to make a fuss about it.'

'I think the general idea is that you're supposed to be feeling sorry,' Jane said. 'I mean, wasn't your heart – both your hearts – ever moved by pity?'

The telescope eyes swivelled towards her. 'I never wasted my pity on the lowest of the low.'

'Well, you should have,' the Lamb said. 'They have exactly the same feelings as the highest of the high. And if you don't learn that, I don't see how you're ever going to get home.'

Fourteen

BONFIRE

Letter from Lt C. J. Pemberton,
9th Loamshires,
October 1915

Dear All,

This is just a quick note to say I'm alive and in one piece and finally in rest-billets well behind the lines. I'm staying in a farmhouse on the very edge of a village, and it does my soul good to hear hens instead of guns. The weather is golden and sometimes I can ignore the eternal background noise of the heavy howitzers and imagine I'm back at the White House.

Poor old Harper was killed last week. He caught a bullet while out in No Man's Land with a wire-cutting party.

They had to leave him out there, but a couple of us went out to fetch him when things were a bit quieter. He was still alive then, but he died before we could get him to the clearing station. I've written all this to his family. I wanted them to know that he died like the A1 brick he was – his last words were 'don't worry'. He knew that I was with him right up to the end and I was holding his hand (I particularly thought his mother might like to know this).

It's funny that none of you ever met Harper, when he was such a great pal of mine. You'll have to take my word that he was one of the grandest old fellows who ever drew breath. I'm absolutely lost without him and still can't quite believe I'll never see his cheery face again.

As for me, I'm in rude health – don't ever imagine you can send me too much home food.

Toodle-oo

Cyril

THE SORROWFUL NEWS about Harper caused the first serious quarrel between Edie and the Psammead. She couldn't help crying, and one of her tears had splashed down on the cushion where he was sitting.

'It didn't even fall ON him,' she said afterwards. 'Just NEAR him – but he started screaming till I was scared someone would hear. He was horrid about poor Harper and said he couldn't see why I was crying over someone I've never met. I said it's perfectly possible to be sorry about a person you've never met – and we did sort of meet Harper. He was nice, that's all, and I'll jolly well cry for him if I want to.'

It was autumn again and the damp, chilly, gusty weather was making everyone gloomy. Jane had caught two colds one after the other from cycling to school through the swirling brown leaves. The Lamb was spending several unpleasant afternoons a week getting plastered with cold mud on his school's football pitch. The war had been going on for more than a year, and there was no sign of it stopping. Every day the newspapers carried long lists of casualties. At almost every school assembly, the Lamb's headmaster read out the names of old boys who had been killed in action. There were shortages of everything; Father had to struggle to get enough paper to print his magazine, and Mother said she dreamed about finding half decent cuts of meat.

'Look here, you'll have to make it up with the Psammead,' the Lamb said, on the fifth of November. 'You're his favourite. He's cutting me and Jane – whenever I try to dig him out of his sand bath he just burrows in deeper. And Bobs will want to see him.'

Robert had finished his exams and joined the army; he was now 2nd Lieutenant R. Pemberton, and had a week's leave before his regiment went to France. Mother was upset, and said she'd worry about Robert far more than she did about Cyril. Father didn't like it either, but he knew Robert felt he was doing the right thing, and was determined to put a good face on it. They all wanted his leave to be as nice as possible; it would be an awful shame if he missed out on seeing the Psammead.

'Oh, all right, I'll talk to him again.' Edie hadn't been on speakers with him for nearly two weeks, and had secretly been longing for an excuse to make it up; she loved the vain little tyrant with all her heart and had missed him horribly. 'Bring him downstairs.'

There was a fire in the shabby, comfortable old nursery, and their parents were out, so it was quite safe. While the Lamb went up to the attic to fetch the Psammead, Edie put more coals on the fire and stoked it to a blaze – though she was strictly not allowed to do this – to make it specially warm and welcoming.

The Lamb returned, red-faced and empty-handed. 'I can't budge him! He's making himself as heavy as a cannonball!'

'He's still cross,' Edie said.

'Come up and say sorry to him.'

'Me? He's the one who should say sorry!'

'Look here, we both know he's wrong and you're right, but couldn't you just humour him?'

In the end, it was the only thing to do. Edie went up to the attic, bent over the sand bath, and begged the Psammead to come out like a gentleman. 'Please, Psammead! Bobs is coming back today and I know he'll want to see you!'

The mound of sand heaved and shifted, and the Psammead's little head poked up. 'Very well, for Robert's sake I shall forget about the disgraceful things you said about my character.'

Edie picked him up and he was his usual weight again, warm and dry in her arms.

'Time has passed,' the Psammead said. 'I thought the war would be over by now – but it must be getting worse. So Robert has had to leave his parchment and his goose quill and take up a musket.'

'You're ridiculously out of date,' the Lamb said. 'Bobs is the modern sort of scholar, with paper and a fountain pen – and he's taking up a Lee-Enfield rifle, not a musket.'

The Psammead ignored him. 'When I was a desert god, I only turned my scholars into warriors as a last resort – they were far too weedy for any serious fighting.'

★

'Cambridge is more like an army camp than ever these days,' Robert said. 'All the colleges are packed full of chaps in khaki. The minute the exams were over, two chaps from the Engineers moved into my room. And then I was in the army – staying in an identical room in another college. I can't say I'm all that keen on soldiering – I'm not like old Squirrel, who loved messing about with the OTC at school. But it's somehow the only thing to do.'

Robert had arrived home in his splendid new officer's uniform. He immediately changed into one of his baggy, old tweed suits, and was now lounging comfortably on the rug beside the nursery fire as if he'd never been away.

'Mother hoped they wouldn't take you because you wear glasses,' Jane said.

'That might have been true a year ago but they're not so fussy now – and my eyesight isn't that bad.'

'Well, it's very nice to see you,' the Psammead said from his perch on the coal bucket. 'You're just in time to help with burning the traitor – if you can believe it, this frightful fellow was caught trying to blow up Parliament!'

Robert chuckled. 'If you mean Guy Fawkes, that happened several hundred years ago. We're only burning an effigy of him.'

'We made him out of my old school clothes,' the Lamb said. 'And his head's a ball of old papers, so he burns nicely. We wanted to take him to the station and shout "penny for the guy", only Mother says it's common.'

'That's exactly what she said when Lilian Winterbottom and I wanted to do it,' Robert said.

The Psammead sighed impatiently. 'What odd customs you have! Why not just burn a fresh traitor? They always make a lovely blaze – though if you want a really sweet smell, it's best to burn a saint. The scent is delicious, like charred roses.'

Robert burst out laughing. 'Psammead, you're the utter limit – how many saints have you burned?'

'I didn't say I burned saints,' the Psammead said coldly. 'If you must know, I was taking shelter in a hole in Rome when the emperor suddenly built the Colosseum on top of me. And he was constantly burning Christians – it was a big crowd-puller.'

'We don't burn anyone nowadays,' Robert said. 'We're a lot more civilised than ancient Romans.'

'Ha! That's what you think! The Romans would never have had a stupid war like this, where everybody gets killed and nobody wins anything worth having. During my days as a god—'

'Oh, here we go!' the Lamb groaned.

'I'm giving you the benefit of my vast experience! When I was a god, the biggest mistake I made was trying to start a war that none of my people wanted to fight. After the first doomed attack they simply lost heart.' His mouth scrunched up painfully. 'But something in this memory is as prickly and uncomfortable as a sand bath full of bees! No! Stop it!' The agitated sand fairy folded himself into a tight, hard ball.

'Crikey,' Robert said. 'What's he doing?'

'He's probably remembered another of his old crimes,' Edie said, picking up the Psammead. 'That always upsets him.'

A motor horn tooted at the end of the lane.

'Good egg – that'll be the Winterbottoms.' Robert jumped up. 'Time to light that beauteous bonfire.'

The Lamb, Edie and Jane, with some help from Father and Field, had built a magnificent ten-foot bonfire on a scrubby patch of land beyond the stables, where the smoke couldn't get into the curtains and make Mother complain that the house reeked of kippers. Father still enjoyed Guy Fawkes Night, and this year he'd made a special trip to a Chinese shop in Limehouse to buy firecrackers and Roman candles. To make the occasion yet more special he had invited the Winterbottoms.

Edie bundled the Psammead in her skirt and ran up to the attic. He sank into the sand bath until only his eyes and mouth stuck out.

'I sent that scribe into danger, but a warrior maiden walked into the jaws of death to save him,' he said, in a small, quiet voice.

'Whatever you're talking about, I can tell you're

sorry now.' Edie smoothed the sand as if tucking in a sheet. 'I'm sure that's what's making you so uncomfortable.'

'Being sorry is very BOTHERSOME!' the Psammead hissed, and sank into invisibility.

Fifteen

A CONFESSION

THE PARENTS HAD COME OUT into the hall, to open the front door and spill out welcoming light for their guests.

'Good old Winterbums!' Father said.

'Charlie!' Mother said.

'What?'

'How can I stop the children doing it if you keep doing it?'

'All right – good old WinterBEHINDS, then.'

The Lamb was delighted to see his best friend from school (though it was a little sickening that they were supposed to address each other as 'Hilary' and 'Arthur' out of school hours), and they all liked Winterbum's big sister Lilian. She was a large, loud, laughing girl, who had been at school with Anthea;

Father jokily called her 'Airy-Fairy Lilian', after a famous poem, because she was anything but airy-fairy and always beat him at tennis.

'We're very lucky to have Lilian with us,' Winterbum's mother said. 'She only has forty-eight hours' leave. I think it's quite dreadful to make girls drive ambulances when they're needed at home.'

Lilian – once the local tomboy and Robert's hoydenish partner-in-crime – had left home to work as an ambulance driver.

'Stow it, Mother,' Lilian said cheerfully. She was wearing her Red Cross uniform of dark blue coat and skirt and felt hat. 'The wounded need me more than you do.'

Her mother said young people didn't listen to their parents anymore.

'When did they ever?' Father said. 'Mine wanted me to be a vicar! Here, Lilian – I'm trusting the box of bangers to your airy-fairy yet capable hands.'

The two mothers and Winterbum's father didn't want to see the bonfire, and shut themselves in the sitting room. Everyone else pulled on coats and hats and trooped out into the darkness, laughing and stumbling in the shifting, unreliable light of torches and lanterns.

'Mother can't stop moaning, but I just let it wash over me,' Lilian was telling Jane. 'It's the sheerest bliss to be back at home in a soft bed – our hostel in London isn't too bad but the mattresses are agony. Most of my life is spent shivering in railway stations, waiting for the hospital trains to bring in the wounded. And then you should see me fighting my way through the London traffic, though people are usually pretty good about making way for an ambulance.'

'She's allowed to mess about with the engine,' Winterbum told the Lamb. 'Before the war, she said she wanted to be a blacksmith, but now she wants to be a motor mechanic. It puts Mother in a terrible flap.'

They walked around the corner of the stables, and saw that the magnificent bonfire already had a heart of flame, thanks to Mr Field. The dry wood caught quickly and the fire lit them all with a dramatic, deep orange light.

Father – as excited as anyone – shouted, 'Death to the traitor!' and threw a handful of bangers and firecrackers at the Guy Fawkes perched on the bonfire's summit. Robert lit the Roman candles, which shot out great fountains of red and green sparks.

Robert and Lilian had been great friends as children,

and the two of them laughed and horsed about as if they'd never grown up. The air was filled with smoke that made everyone's eyes sting. In the darkness Edie held tight to Jane's hand; the flashes reminded her of the trench where they had seen Cyril, and the shapeless 'Guy' looked disturbingly human in the flickering light of the flames.

And then it suddenly turned into a figure made of flames, a figure with a squat body and long arms and legs.

'Crikey,' Jane said, 'it's the Psammead!'

Edie was too horrified to make a sound. She stared as the fiery figure grew larger and larger, until the entire bonfire looked as if it had turned into a huge, blazing Psammead. Burning branches crashed down around it, and Jane pulled Edie out of the stinging sparks; the air was full of them, like a blizzard of angry fireflies.

'Stand back there!' Lilian shouted. 'Bobs – start pumping!'

Lilian and Robert had grabbed the stirrup pump from the stable yard. Robert pumped for all he was worth, while Lilian directed a jet of water at the fire.

'NO!' Edie screamed, horrified. 'Not water! He'll get wet – he'll be ill!'

'Shhh!' Jane gently shook her. 'Keep quiet –
honestly, it's all right!'

Edie dared to look, and to her great relief the
flaming sand fairy had vanished and it was just an
ordinary bonfire again, partly black and smoking
where it had blazed out of control.

'Well played, you two,' Father said breathlessly.
'Lilian, you went at that like Queen Boadicea – Bobs,
old boy, well done for knowing where to find the
stirrup pump – which is more than I did!'

'You built the fire too tall and narrow, that's all,'
Robert said, equally breathless.

'Yes, and you stopped it falling right on top of Jane
and Baby – are you all right, girlies? Not burned to
crisps?'

'We're fine.' Jane nudged Edie, who was still trembling.

'And where are the boys?'

'Here!' The Lamb and his friend stepped out of
the shadows. Their faces in the flickering light of the
bonfire were striped with soot.

'Look here, Bobs,' Father said, 'someone sent me a
pair of excellent tickets for *The Mikado* at the Savoy
Theatre tomorrow. I'm giving them to you, on the
condition that you take Lilian, as a thank-you.'

'Thanks, Dad.' Robert grinned at Lilian. 'What about it, old bean?'

'You know, I'd love to,' Lilian said. 'It's the last night of my leave and Mother won't like me going out – but Mother doesn't like anything I do at the moment.'

'That's settled then.'

'I say, it'll be a lark to wear a frock again – it's ages since I dressed up as a girl!'

★

The moment everyone had gone Edie dashed upstairs to the attic to make sure the Psammead was safe; she was very worried that the water had hurt him. It was a great relief to find him dry and sleepy in his sand bath.

'What is it? Why are you digging me out in the middle of the night?'

'You appeared again – you were made of fire, and you grew into a huge burning Psammead.' She picked him up carefully, scrubbed her lips with her sleeve to make sure they were perfectly dry, and dropped a kiss on the top of his head. 'Are you really all right?'

'I was – until you woke me up!' He was grumbling, but didn't object when Edie carried him out of the

190

chilly attic and downstairs to the old nursery, where Robert had revived the dying fire. 'Couldn't this have waited till morning?'

'No,' Jane said. 'I can't go to bed until I know you're not going to burst into flames again.'

'I'm sorry I missed that,' the Lamb said. 'All me and Winterbum saw was a normal bonfire. I bet it happened because of another of your crimes – you'd better make a list of everybody you burned, so you can repent properly.'

'I didn't burn anyone! As I have said before, I was a thrifty tyrant, and burning people takes a lot of fuel.'

Robert was laughing. 'It doesn't sound as if your repentance has got very far – you're still as vain as a peacock.'

'But he truly has got kinder,' Edie said eagerly. 'And he admits he was wrong sometimes.'

'I can't tell you the meaning of the fire,' the Psammead said. 'I am undergoing certain uncomfortable feelings – it feels quite a lot like trapped wind, but Edie says it's remorse.' He sighed heavily. 'If you must know, while you were all outside, I had a troubling dream about a young scholar in my court. His name was Mapeth.'

'And I expect you did something bad to him.' Edie was sad but resigned.

The Psammead winced. 'Let me go back to my sand bath now. Tomorrow I must dictate a full confession to your professor. I'm sure he'll be able to fill in the gaps.'

> *Letter from the Psammead to Professor J. Knight and Mr E. Haywood (dictated to Jane)*

Dear scribes,

Greetings from the Powerful One. I seek enlightenment.

Last night Jane and Edie saw a fire change into a giant burning sand fairy. But I can't remember anything to do with fire. I was having quite a different sort of memory – a dream about a young man named Mapeth.

Frankly, I don't come out of this well.

Mapeth was a brilliant young scholar in my desert kingdom. He did my accounts and also wrote very good worship songs all about me. When the High Priestess brought out her book of poems I was extremely jealous and longed to produce some poems of my own. Of course, I couldn't write them myself – so I made Mapeth write them and I passed them off as mine. They were lovely poems and they were very popular – and then it was HER turn to be jealous of me!

But I didn't want anyone to know the real author, so I made Mapeth join the army. He was weedy and skinny and very short-sighted, and I was sure he'd be killed almost at once – I sent him to the place my soldiers called the Valley of No Return, the point being that nobody did. Mapeth was horribly wounded but he did not die. One of the warrior maidens from the temple was in love with him; she followed him into the dreadful valley, plucked him out of the jaws of death and nursed him back to health. Edie thinks this is highly romantic. Human girls are so sentimental.

The fire still puzzles me; perhaps you can find out what it means. I really can't remember anything else. But I MUST remember or I can't move on to the green fields all covered with white blossoms that I have glimpsed in my dreams.

These green fields are not in my past – might they be my final refuge?

*You'll be glad to hear I'm pretty well, despite the
shockingly damp weather.*

Yours graciously

*HE WHO MUST BE WORSHIPPED AND
OBEYED*

The Last Psammead

Sixteen

BARTIMEUS

O<small>N</small> C<small>HRISTMAS</small> E<small>VE</small> M<small>OTHER</small> <small>SAID</small>, 'Last year I was missing only one of my children. This year it's three of them – Cyril and Robert in France and Anthea at her wretched hospital.' There were tears in her eyes. 'I feel as if I'm giving them up one after the other, like the mother of the Maccabees in the poem.'

'It can't go on much longer,' Father said.

'But that's exactly what he said last year,' the Lamb said later, when he and Edie had gone up to the attic to escape the unChristmassy gloom; nobody was in the mood for festivity. Jane, though her term had ended, was shut in her bedroom revising for an exam coming up in January. The Winterbottoms were being visited by grandparents, which meant that Winterbum wasn't available for cycling with the Lamb. 'I don't think the war's EVER going to stop. I think it'll go on until I'm old enough to be called up. In which case, what's the point of me learning Latin?'

'It's going to be horrid without Panther and the boys,' Edie said sadly. 'I'm not even looking forward to hanging up my stocking this year.'

'Another very strange custom,' the Psammead said. 'I've been on this earth for thousands of years and I'll never understand you humans – putting gifts inside old socks!'

He had come out of his sand bath to sit in Edie's lap while she brushed his fur.

'Father says his socks aren't big enough,' she told him. 'He ties strings around the legs of his long underpants and hangs those up instead. And Mother says don't be vulgar, but she laughs as much as anyone. I don't know if he'll do it this year.' She stroked the Psammead's head. 'If you weren't here, I don't know what we'd do.'

'You're very kind, Edie, but I must remind you that I'm not actually supposed to be here. I thought I'd be gone in a matter of days! I do WISH the universe would hurry up with my next lesson in repentance.'

A silence hung in the air for a few seconds. The Lamb and Edie had learned to recognise the breathless feeling they got when they were about to be whisked away by one of the Psammead's mad wishes.

'This is more like it!' the Lamb said, brightening. 'You haven't scored a single wish for weeks!'

'Where are we going? I'm not ready – ow!' Edie flung her arms around the Psammead.

He had wished for another lesson from the universe, and the universe chose to drop them in a narrow room, lit by a single gaslight. There were two beds with iron frames, one table, two hard chairs, and a tiny fireplace. The window was high up in the wall and it had bars on the outside.

'We seem to be in some kind of penal institution,' the Psammead said. 'Possibly a prison.'

'No, it's not a prison.' The Lamb's eyes had got used to the sudden light and he'd taken a proper look. 'Prison cells don't have cushions, or photographs in silver frames – crikey!' He pointed at a photograph beside one of the beds. 'Edie, it's us! It's the picture Jane took of you and me with the Psammead – only he didn't come out.'

On the surface it was an ordinary photograph of the Lamb and Edie on a sofa, but if you looked hard, the cushion between them was slightly dented;

this was the only sign that the Psammead had been posing with them.

'I simply refuse to have anything to do with those ghastly photo things,' the Psammead sniffed. 'It's forbidden to make such lifelike images of a god.'

'And the other picture's Mother,' Edie said. 'We must be in Anthea's hospital!'

At that moment the door opened and two young nurses burst into the room in fits of excited giggles. They were both carrying large cardboard boxes. It took Edie a few seconds to realise that one of them was Anthea; she was so unfamiliar in her blue dress and starched white cap and apron.

'This is more like it – a sight of good old Panther!' The Lamb was beaming. 'And that's the box we sent off to her yesterday!'

'I just wish she knew we were here,' Edie said. 'Psammead, can't I hug her?'

'No,' the Psammead said. 'And if you start crying again I won't let you carry me. Now, let's watch.'

The other girl was short and plump, with dark hair and a pretty, rosy, dimpled face.

'That's Olive, the dentist's daughter,' Edie said, cheering up. 'Doesn't she look nice?'

Both the boxes were full of Christmas presents. The two girls took out the packages one by one and piled them on their hard white beds.

'What a lovely, glorious heap of loot!' Olive sighed.

'My presents smell of home – it does feel awful not being at home on Christmas Eve,' Anthea said. She was smiling but her voice wobbled.

'Chin up, old thing,' Olive said. 'Look here, I know we agreed not to open anything until we come off night shift, but let's each have one present now.'

'Should we? It's not Christmas yet.'

'I don't care. I need something to get me into the right spirit.'

'Just one, then.'

'If she's got any sense she'll open my stuffed dates,' the Lamb said. 'I know she likes them.'

Olive picked up one of her holly-sprigged parcels and shook it. 'Oh, joy – the rattle of mint humbugs!' She tore the paper off a tin with a picture on the lid of Ripon Cathedral, stuffed one of the striped mints into her mouth, and handed one to Anthea. 'Good old Auntie Flo!'

They giggled again at each other's bulging cheeks.

'I'll have to finish this quickly,' Anthea said. 'I can't

face the Ponting if I'm reeking of humbugs – she's such a joyless old harridan.'

'That's the ward sister she doesn't like,' Edie told the Psammead.

'Thank you, Edie, I remember her from Anthea's letters.'

'Now it's your turn – quick, we've not got long,' Olive said.

'Oh, I don't know!' Anthea picked up a light, flat parcel. 'This one – it's from my little sister Edie.'

Edie beamed with pride. 'I do hope she likes it. It took me nearly half a term of needlework classes.' She had made Anthea a lavender sachet to put in her handkerchief drawer.

Anthea carefully took off the paper. 'How lovely!'

'The little darling,' Olive said. 'She's embroidered something in cross stitch – is that a monkey?'

Anthea had been on the verge of crying again, but now she was laughing; the 'monkey' was Edie's attempt to embroider a picture of the Psammead.

'Monkey, indeed!' the Psammead huffed crossly.

'She's never seen a sand fairy,' the Lamb pointed out.

'I suppose not – it's a shame she can't appreciate the beauty of Edie's priceless tapestry.'

'I don't care what it is – as far as I'm concerned this is a priceless tapestry!' Anthea said.

'She heard!' gasped Edie.

'Perhaps,' the Psammead said, 'in some dark corner of her mind. I'm delighted to see her, though I don't understand what I'm supposed to be looking at. Why haven't we gone home yet?'

Olive glanced at the nurse's watch she wore on the front of her stiff white apron. 'We'd better get going, you know we're not meant to be here.' She turned off the gas and they hurried out of the room.

The Lamb and Edie walked through the wall after them.

'I like doing this,' the Lamb said. 'It feels like cold water running down the middle of my bones.'

'Yes – that's exactly why I DON'T like it.' Edie held the Psammead tighter.

They followed Anthea and Olive down a dark stone staircase and along a corridor to a room full of numbered pegs. The two young nurses grabbed their blue cloaks and flung them on. They ran through a pair of doors and out into the freezing night air.

'Oh!' moaned the Psammead. 'Why am I still here?

Oh, universe – or whatever you are – can't we at least wait in the warm till they come back?'

'Don't be so wet,' the Lamb said scornfully. 'This is all part of your repentance. You're just like Scrooge in the story – you have to pay attention to what the spirits are telling you.'

'Who?'

'Never mind – we're losing them.'

Anthea and Olive were trotting briskly down the path between the nurses' home and the main hospital building. They went into the hospital through a door at the side, and slowed down in the empty corridor.

Olive checked her watch. 'Good-oh – we made it with five minutes to spare.'

They hung up their cloaks and, because the corridor was empty, Olive did a few jaunty dance steps.

Somewhere nearby voices started to sing 'O Little Town of Bethlehem'. The Lamb and Edie saw the choir as they went past the open door of one of the hospital wards. A vicar with white hair was conducting a group of elderly singers around a large Christmas tree covered with candles. The patients wore paper crowns, as well as their bandages. Most of them were smoking, and a couple puffed on pipes.

'Crikey,' Olive said, 'Christmas is breaking out with a vengeance! Good luck with Ponting.' She ran along the corridor.

The Lamb and Edie followed their big sister into another ward, which was shadowy and silent. Anthea smoothed her apron, knocked on a door, and went into a glassed-in office that looked like a small greenhouse.

'Good evening, Sister.'

'Well, well!' the Psammead said. 'So this is the famous Sister Ponting! I expected her to look more like a wicked witch.'

Sister Ponting was writing something at her desk. Edie shivered at the stern expression that came into her eyes when she glanced up at Anthea. She was old, with grey hair and glasses on a gilt chain.

'Ah, Pemberton.' She frowned at her watch. 'Nearly two minutes late.'

'Sorry, Sister.'

'You are not running a race. I expect my nurses to arrive with at least a few minutes to spare.'

'Yes, Sister.'

'You're not much use if you're panting like a race horse!'

'No, Sister.'

Sister Ponting put the lid on her pen and stood up. 'We had some new arrivals this afternoon – all gas cases – and the doctor says most of them won't last the night. I'm putting you in charge of the boy in side ward B.'

'Yes, Sister.'

'We put him in the side ward because he was upsetting the other patients. Your job will be to keep him quiet and calm.'

'Yes, Sister.'

'What a horrid woman,' Edie said hotly. 'She sounds just like Miss Bligh at my school!'

Sister Ponting left her office with Anthea close behind her – and no idea that she was also being followed by two invisible children and a sand fairy.

There were no carol-singers in this ward, and no Christmas tree. It was quiet and the lights were turned low, and all the patients lay very still under their white covers. Sister Ponting led Anthea into a small side room, where another young nurse sat beside the only bed.

'Any change?' Sister asked.

'He woke at about four,' the nurse said softly. 'I think he was delirious – he wanted steak and kidney pie. And he kept trying to say something I couldn't make out. But he's quietened down now.'

'Thank you, nurse,' Sister said. 'You may go.'

The other nurse left the room, giving a quick, tired smile to Anthea.

'This is Private Grant,' Sister said. 'If he rests properly now, he has a fighting chance of surviving the next twenty-four hours. The gas has burned his lungs, eyes and mouth. You mustn't let him talk, and he mustn't be agitated. If there's a crisis, or you think he's sinking, ring the bell.'

'Yes, Sister.' Anthea sat down in the chair beside the bed.

'Sinking? Does that mean he's going to die?' The Psammead was indignant. 'Well, that's a nice thing to show me!'

'Shut up!' the Lamb hissed.

'Why? He can't hear me.'

'I don't care! It just doesn't feel right to make a noise here.'

Though they knew they couldn't be heard, the Lamb and Edie crept to the bed on tiptoe. Private Grant's head and eyes were wrapped in layers and layers of gauze bandages, and his lips were cracked and sore.

'This is a very dreadful sight,' the Psammead muttered.

The patient's sore lips moved painfully and he made a thin, wheezing, rattling sound whenever he drew a breath.

Anthea took his hand. 'It's all right,' she said softly. 'You can't see me, but I'm Nurse Pemberton and I'm here to watch over you. Please don't try to talk.'

'Eyes!' he whispered.

'Are you in pain? Squeeze my hand for yes.'

'Bartimeus,' he whispered, with effort.

'Who? What on earth is he on about?' The Psammead's ears were rigid from listening extra hard. 'It's no good showing me if I don't understand!'

'I think I do,' the Lamb said. 'The Bigguns had a guinea pig called Bartimeus. Father named him after a chap in the Bible, because he was blind and so was this chap – blind Bartimeus, who sat by the roadside begging.'

'Poor thing,' Edie said. 'How dreadful to be blind – but maybe he won't be when they take off the bandages.'

'I can't bear any more,' the Psammead said in a shaking voice. 'I'm getting very tired of this and I'm LEAVING!'

He shrilled his complaint with such confidence that both children braced themselves for a swift return to the attic.

But they were still here, watching Anthea's face in the soft shadows, and listening to the young man's agonised breathing.

'Pooh!' the Psammead muttered. 'I didn't think it would be as hard as this.'

Private Grant's lips moved again.

'You really mustn't talk, it's so bad for your lungs,' Anthea said. 'Try to lie quietly. Is it better if you can hear me talking?'

He squeezed her hand.

'All right, I'll talk to you for a few minutes, until you fall asleep. Oh dear – what shall I talk about? I can't think of a single thing.' Anthea frowned anxiously, and while she floundered for something to say, the sore lips began to move again. 'Please – you mustn't talk – oh dear!'

'If Anthea could hear me, I'd tell her to pull herself together,' the Psammead said. 'Of course she knows what to talk about – that must be the reason I'm here!'

'I know!' Anthea stopped looking helpless and smiled, as if she'd heard him. 'I'll tell you a story.' Lowering her voice and bending her head closer, she began, 'Once upon a time, there were five children—'

And then the world spun and they were back in the attic.

'Good heavens,' the Psammead murmured, 'for once, I seem to have done something useful.'

Dearest Janey, Lamb, Edie and Psammead,

This is your private letter, not for parental eyes, because it includes a certain sand fairy.

Everyone is doing their best to make a happy Christmas for our poor wounded patients – the entire hospital has been ringing with jollity for days. But I must admit I was feeling pretty blue yesterday – I missed you all so much, and wished like anything I could see E.

It was greatly cheering-up to hear that there was a box for me at the porter's lodge. Thanks so much for all the presents! Jane, the bedsocks are utter heaven – I'm wearing them now because I'm writing this in bed, and it's the first time my feet have been warm for weeks. Lamb, thanks for the box of dates; you know how I love them. And Edie darling, your sachet is simply a marvel. I'm sorry to say that Olive thought the Psammead was a monkey; I hope he's not offended.

And the sight of him must have blown some cheer into my Christmas Eve. I was taking care of a boy who had been very badly gassed. I was ordered to keep him quiet but he kept trying to talk, and I was at my wits' end until I thought of calming him down by telling him a story – naturally, all about the Psammead, the best (and only) story I know. He calmed down like an angel and fell asleep. And he was so much better this morning that Ponting actually uttered the immortal words: 'Well done, Pemberton.' What a turn-up! Tired as I was, I danced all the way back to the nurses' home.

After that, Olive and I opened our wondrous Christmas presents, and had a superb breakfast – bacon! Coffee! Porridge with CREAM! – kindly donated by the local Methodists. Three cheers for them, and for the Church of England ladies who decided to do their bit for the war effort by providing a stupendous lunch for hungry nurses.

In the afternoon there was a big carol service for the patients. Everybody well enough was wheeled in. I was lucky to be pushing a very jolly Welsh sergeant, who has lost both his legs (you can imagine how I thought of E), and kept trying to give me swigs of rum from his flask! He smelled like a plum pudding and I trembled every time he lit a match (he smoked nasty little Woodbine cigarettes at every opportunity) in case he burst into flames. He turned out to have the most beautiful singing voice and it was lovely to hear him.

But here's the best part. When I finally dragged myself off to bed (no night shift tonight – hurrah), I happened to glance at Jane's famous snapshot of Edie plus Lamb plus invisible Psammead – and the Psammead isn't invisible anymore! There he is, sitting on the cushion with a superior expression on his furry face – looking so extraordinary that I had to stifle a shriek and hide the photo in the drawer before Olive saw it.

Dear old Psammead, it does me a world of good to look at you, and think of you in the attic at home, radiating the magic and happiness of the old days when we were all together and life was one long summer afternoon.

I miss all of you dreadfully and hope your Christmas Day was as nice as mine.

Heaps of love and (perfectly dry) kisses

Panther

Seventeen

DOWNFALL

1916

THE LAMB AND EDIE WERE VERY pleased to hear the good news about Anthea's patient. It helped to cheer up a new year that would otherwise have been grey and depressing.

'Obviously that soldier got so much better because I was there,' the Psammead said smugly. 'I'm not used to spreading joy. It feels nicer than spreading misery and terror.'

1916 was the third year of the war, and also the third year of the Psammead. He had been living in the attic for so many months that Edie had gradually made it more comfortable and homelike. She had dragged an ancient sofa over to the Psammead's sand bath, heaped it with musty cushions, and sneaked in a small oil lamp (no grown-up knew about this). Jane and the Lamb visited as often as they could, but they were both busy with schoolwork, and it was still Edie who spent most time with him.

'Mother is always at her committees and the others are always out or working,' she wrote to Anthea. 'And if it wasn't for the dear old Psammead, I'd be rather lonely. He's in a good mood at the moment, and he even helps with my homework.'

Thanks to the Psammead, Edie came top in Latin.

'Naturally I'm fluent in Latin,' he told her. 'I had to put up with the Roman Empire for centuries. It was extremely noisy – after the amphitheatre, I moved my lodgings to a public bathhouse, but that was even worse. Why must humans sing when they're washing themselves?'

Though he insisted he knew everything, the Psammead wasn't as useful in other subjects – his French was medieval, and his geography and history were stuck thousands of years in the past. Edie was happiest when they simply chatted and he allowed her to ask him questions. He enjoyed talking about his distant origins.

'My first long spell in hiding was after the meteor

that killed off the dinosaurs. Personally, I was glad to see the back of those great, lumbering, clumsy reptiles. They smelled AWFUL, and left vast DROPPINGS one was forever falling into.'

But there were no more adventures. Weeks and weeks passed in dull normality, without a whiff of magic to distract them from the war. At the Lamb's school, the list of masters and old boys who had been killed in action was growing so fast that they had to put up a new honours board in the assembly hall because the old one was full. Two more girls in Edie's class wore black dresses because they had lost their fathers. Mother had grey hairs now, and counted the days between the boys' letters.

And there were shortages of things people had always taken for granted, such as bread, which you were supposed to cut down on because it was the staple food of the very poor. Father, though officially on the poor's side, made this sacrifice very unwillingly.

'Dammit, I am not eating this cardboard imitation of toast – or this deformed fish,' he said at lunchtime.

'It's a meatless day,' Mother said. 'Everyone in the entire country is eating deformed fish.'

'Well, it's frightful. I'd like to force-feed the Kaiser

213

with all the cabbages and potatoes I've had to eat since he started this war.'

'I've noticed something,' Edie told Jane later. 'The Psammead doesn't talk about leaving anymore. But I don't think he's happy – he says he likes talking to me because it takes his mind off the clamour of eternity. Whatever that means.'

'You know my theory,' Jane said. 'I think we need the Psammead at least as much as he needs us. That's what's keeping him here, whether he likes it or not. I don't think we'll see the back of him until the war ends.'

★

In the spring of 1916 there were two momentous events at home. The Lamb turned thirteen, which was splendidly better than being twelve. His parents gave him the wristwatch of his dreams and Mrs Field made a cake with icing (sugar was hard to come by, but she said she had her connections).

And Ernie had an article published in the *Daily Express*. It was a very funny article about everyday life in the trenches, called 'Top Ten Gripes of the

Common Soldier'. Jane, the Lamb and Edie took it up to the attic to read it to the Psammead.

'I don't quite understand all the jokes,' Edie said, 'but isn't Ernie clever? I hope Anthea's seen it.'

'I'll send it to her, in case she missed it,' Jane said. 'I heard Father saying how good it was, and I told him right out it was by the same Ernest Haywood we visited in hospital. Mother must've told him her suspicions about Anthea because he played with his moustache and went "Hmmm" a bit. But then he said, "Dammit, it's a terrific piece. If you're still in touch, tell him to write to me at the *Citizen*." And then he said, "Don't tell your mother." So she definitely does have suspicions. But I sent a postcard to Ernie straight away. Wouldn't it be topping if Father published something by him?'

The Psammead's eyes swivelled haughtily. 'The one-legged scribe is wasting time – he should be writing his great work about me.'

'Typical!' Jane said. 'Psammead, you're the most self-centred being on earth. The one-legged scribe needs to earn a living, and he won't make much money out of Jimmy's book.'

'Don't be mean to him! He's only self-centred

because he's the last of his kind,' Edie said.

'There speaks the faithful handmaiden,' the Lamb said. 'You'd make allowances for old Sammy if he turned out to be Attila the Hun.'

'I would not! I'm just saying, you can see why he's so taken up with the book – Jimmy hasn't found out anything new for ages.'

'We should take one of our Saturday trips to see him,' Jane said. 'We've got the perfect excuse to go to Old Nurse's – the poor old thing's been ill, which means Father will give us the train fares because he feels guilty about not going himself. And it'll do me good to get away from the eternal argument.'

Jane was fresh from yet another row with Mother about going to medical school. She had lost her temper and called Mother 'hopelessly old-fashioned', and Mother had cried because she thought Jane would end her days as a wizened old spinster.

'I don't see why you have to keep bringing it up,' the Lamb said. 'It makes everyone so dashed cross.'

'Mother wants votes for women, but she doesn't believe a woman can ever be a proper doctor. She wants me to "get it all out of my system" by treating children in the East End who have ringworm. I said

I wasn't some parish visitor do-gooding type and I wanted to perform amputations.'

Edie shuddered. 'You couldn't!'

'Of course I could. It isn't even particularly complicated.'

'There's a lot of blood,' the Psammead said. 'If you're not careful it gets everywhere.'

'You furry old fiend!' The Lamb burst out laughing. 'How many arms and legs have you chopped off in your time?'

'I didn't do that sort of menial work, thank you,' the sand fairy said in a dignified voice. 'I don't think any of you realise quite how great I was once. And if you're going to wrap me in a napkin again, please ensure that it is PERFECTLY DRY – last time I came dangerously close to a lethal smear of rhubarb jam.'

⋆

'I don't know where we'd be without young Ernie,' Old Nurse said. 'He does all our fetching and carrying – takes the coal upstairs to save Ivy's back, and all those trays.'

She had been ill with pleurisy, and now sat in an

armchair beside the kitchen fire, her legs covered with an eiderdown. Jane, Edie and the Lamb had come straight down to the basement to have tea with her, but they were itching to get upstairs. The Psammead was in the basket, and he'd been full of complaints all day; none of them trusted him to stay quiet.

'The Professor's out at the museum today,' Old Nurse said. 'Ernie's here working – I think the two of them have had a bit of a falling-out.'

This was very surprising and they all raised their eyebrows at each other.

'The ungrateful scribe has turned on his master!' a muffled voice in the basket cried.

They all cringed, but Old Nurse was busy chewing cake and didn't hear him.

'What do you mean – they've quarrelled?' Jane asked.

'That's what it sounded like, dear. The whole house heard Professor Knight shouting, "Truth is sacred!" and then storming out.'

'But old Jimmy would be utterly lost without Ernie,' the Lamb said when they were hurrying upstairs. 'She must've got her wires crossed.'

Behind the door of the Professor's study they heard the brisk pecking of a typewriter. Edie knocked.

'Come in!' Ernie was at the desk, which was unusually tidy. 'Blimey – I forgot you lot were coming!' He was embarrassed. 'It's just me today. The Professor sends his apologies.'

'The old crone says you had a falling-out.' The Psammead's cross voice floated from the basket. 'I shall be most displeased if you've killed him.'

The Lamb snorted with laughter.

'Don't call poor Old Nurse a "crone",' Jane said. 'And of course Ernie hasn't killed the Professor – tell him, for goodness sake.'

'The Prof's alive and well,' Ernie said. 'And as you very well know, I wouldn't hurt a hair of his blessed old head. But Mrs Taylor's right, we've had a disagreement.'

'About me?' The Psammead's head popped over the rim of the basket.

Ernie sighed, obviously uncomfortable. 'Yes, in a way. It was about that book the Prof's writing.'

'MY book,' said the Psammead, 'in which the TRUTH of the sand fairy is revealed to the nations.'

'Well, that's just it,' Ernie said. 'It's the one thing we can't agree about. The Professor wants to present

219

his findings as real history. I mean, I know it is real history – but when it's written down it just looks barmy. This was the last straw.'

He handed a sheet of paper to Jane, who read it aloud. 'This book is worshipfully dedicated to the mighty PSAMMEAD, former god of the Akkadian desert, with humble thanks for all the help he has given to the authors.'

'Crikey,' the Lamb said. 'I see what you mean.'

'I don't – what's wrong with it?' Edie said.

'Nobody will believe a word of it,' Jane said.

'Nothing's wrong with it, exactly.' Ernie shot a cautious look at the Psammead. 'It's just not quite the ticket for a serious work of scholarship. I suggested he should call it something like *Myths of the Ancient Near East*, or *Legends of a Lost Civilisation*. But he went berserk and said I had no respect for the truth.'

'I'm not surprised,' the Psammead said. 'I've never been so insulted in my considerable life! Do I LOOK like a myth?'

'Not to me – but that's what people will assume you are. You don't get books about the Greek gods containing dedications to Zeus, with thanks for all his help, do you?'

'I'm glad people don't know you're real,' Edie said. 'You wouldn't be safe if everybody knew about you.' One of her great fears was that the Psammead would somehow fall into the wrong hands, which was why she worried so much about keeping him secret. 'Ernie's only trying to protect you.'

Ernie smiled at her, his face reddening a little. 'Yes, that was part of it. I can't stand the thought of people finding out about you, and turning you into a fairground attraction. But I'm afraid my real reason is more selfish. I've worked hard to pull the Prof's book into shape and I want it to be published – if we put it in the right way, his discoveries will cause a sensation. But if we do it his way, we'll be a laughing stock. I can't afford to ruin my career before it's even started!'

They all knew that if Ernie's writing was successful he would have enough money to support a wife, and then he might be able to marry Anthea.

'So you've nearly finished my book.' The Psammead looked over the edge of the basket at the pile of paper beside the typewriter. 'I see you're working on it now.'

'Er – no,' Ernie said, turning redder. 'That's something of my own. My newspaper work is keeping me pretty busy these days.'

'Did you write to our father?' Edie asked.

'Not yet – it wouldn't be right when he doesn't know about me and Anthea.'

The door opened suddenly and the Professor burst into the room, scattering pieces of paper. 'Haywood, I've got it! How could I have been so obtuse?'

'Look here,' Ernie said, 'I was out of order this morning, and I'm sorry.'

'What? Oh, never mind all that – I'm the one who should apologise – but this is too exciting—' Jimmy was breathless and had the dazed, dreamy look that came over him when he was thinking about the Psammead. 'I've had a new idea about how to read the fragment of carving in Minsk.' He blinked and smiled at the three children and the Psammead. 'Hello, what a delightful – oh, but I was expecting you, wasn't I?'

'Yes, and we've got the postcard to prove it. Do shake hands with Ernie,' Jane said.

'Hmm?'

'You had a blazing row,' the Lamb reminded him.

'Hmm? Oh, great heavens, I nearly forgot! My dear Haywood—' The Professor grabbed Ernie's hand and shook it violently. 'Forgive me, I behaved like an absolute old fool! Now be a good chap and dig out my Russian portfolio.' He bowed to the Psammead. 'Oh Gracious One, I have searched high and low to answer the questions you posed in your letter about the fire – and now another piece has fallen into place.'

'More murdering, I suppose,' the Lamb said cheerfully.

Ernie, nearly as excited as the Professor, pulled a cardboard folder from one of the heaps. It was stuffed with scraps of paper, dull old photographs, and a rubbing of the mysterious Russian stone. 'Not murders – this one's about a huge, hairy tyran. What did you find?'

'It was staring us in the face, my boy – try reading this symbol as "Downfall",' the Professor said,

'Downfall?' The Psammead twitched uneasily. 'That has an uncomfortable sting of familiarity – dear Edie, please don't think less of me when you see that my going out was so much less glorious than my coming in!'

Edie lifted him out of the basket. 'I haven't a clue what you're talking about, but you know I'll never think less of you.'

'Here's the rubbing of the stone.' Ernie spread the large, thin sheet of paper on the desk.

'Don't bother to read it out – I'll give you the gist of it.' The Psammead let out a long, quivering sigh. 'I have to remember now, whether I like it or not. Your bonfire was the heaviest possible hint.'

'Well?' The Lamb was impatient.

The Psammead sat up straight. 'Yes, this stone tells the story of my downfall.' He pulled in his eyes and wrapped his gangling arms and legs around his little blob of a body. 'They burned me at the stake.'

'Oh no – you poor darling!' Edie cried, horrified.

'But the stone says the people rose up against a gigantic monster,' Ernie said. 'And you're hardly gigantic.'

'I was once,' the Psammead said, with another long sigh. 'Hasn't it ever struck any of you that I'm rather small to be a god? In the days of my godhood I was fifteen cubits tall and my limbs were as massive as trees. The fire didn't kill me – I shrank to the size I am today and made a cunning escape down a drain.'

'I like you this size,' Edie said warmly. 'And it makes you much easier to hide – if you'd stayed big, you'd never fit in our tin bath.'

'So you still had control over your magic in those days?' Jane said.

'Unfortunately not – it had nothing to do with my magic,' the Psammead said. 'I shrank to the size of my own popularity, then I was forced into hiding, and I've been in hiding ever since. I'd still be fast asleep at this moment – if you children hadn't woken me up all those years ago in 1902.'

'I say, don't blame us,' the Lamb said. 'We didn't ask you to pop out of our gravel pit.'

Ernie had been writing rapidly in a notebook. 'The children might've woken you with the power of their imagination. It must be very strong when the kids love stories as much as this lot do.'

'No, I think it's simpler than that,' Jane said thoughtfully. 'I think you were attracted to us because we were happy and we loved each other. It sounds like a small thing, but I can see now that it's the biggest thing in the world. That's why you came back to help us when the war broke us apart.'

Eighteen

A LONG, LONG TRAIL

Letter from Lt Cyril Pemberton,
Somewhere in France,
to Miss Mabel Harper,
Oswestry, Shropshire,
May 1916

Dear Miss Harper,

Your letter was waiting for me in a bundle at HQ, which explains why I've taken such a long time to reply. It was topping to hear from you – on paper you sound just like good old Geoffrey. I've missed that bright Harper outlook on the world; I think about him every day. Of course, it's a thousand times worse for his family and I think about you too.

If your trip to London happens to fall in the first two weeks of June, you'll coincide with my leave; let me take you out to tea, and we can share our memories of the dear old boy. You'll be surprised to hear how much I know about you.

Your favourite scent is lilac.

Your favourite colour is rose-pink.

Your favourite song is 'There's a Long, Long Trail A-Winding'.

You have a scar on your right foot from where your brother pushed you out of a tree house.

And I daresay you know all sorts of hideous things about me, but please overlook them.

Yours sincerely,

Cyril Pemberton

IN THE SECOND WEEK OF JUNE it was sports day at the Lamb's school. This was a grand occasion, like a garden party. Besides the races and gymnastic displays, there was a brass band and a striped tea tent, and the ladies wore huge hats laden with feathers and silk flowers. This year felt particularly festive;

the weather was glorious and all the children were together again – Cyril and Robert both had leave and Anthea had been allowed time off from the hospital.

Mother and Father went to talk to the headmaster. The six children strolled across the sunny, crowded lawn, often halting so that Cyril and Robert could shake hands with their old schoolfriends. Cyril and Robert were both in uniform; there was khaki everywhere. The brass band played a jolly selection from *The Gondoliers*, families spread picnic blankets in the meadow next to the sports field, and the war seemed very far away. Edie strolled beside the Lamb, feeling grown up and elegant in her best, white silk dress that she'd just inherited from Jane, and the beautiful gold locket Cyril had given her two days ago for her eleventh birthday. The Lamb was also very smart in his dark red blazer and straw hat, ready to cheer Winterbum on in the hurdles.

'Watch out,' Robert said, 'it's old MacTavish.'

Mr MacTavish, the Lamb's ancient, grey-bearded teacher, hurried over to shake the hands of his former pupils. 'Well, well – a full complement of Pembertons! Very good to see you all! Isn't this a splendid occasion? And isn't the weather marvellous?'

'I wish everybody didn't have to be so cheerful all

the time,' Cyril said when the old man had gone to shake hands with someone else. 'It seems absurd, when half the world's in khaki and the other half's in black – you feel as if you're being patted on the back for not being dead yet.'

'Don't,' Anthea murmured. 'We notice it too, Squirrel darling, though nobody says anything – all the empty spaces.'

They were quiet for a moment, listening to the jaunty music of the band. Cyril had seemed much older when he came home this time; he was quieter, and he smoked cigars after dinner with Father, like a complete grown-up. Robert, on the other hand, wanted as much fun and silliness as possible.

'Perhaps it's all coming to an end at last,' Jane said. 'Everyone's talking about a "Big Push" this summer.'

'Oh yes,' Cyril said. 'I've heard all about the Big Push, and I wish I believed in it – but experience tells me it's more likely to be a small shove.'

They had brought a large picnic basket, filled with sandwiches and a sponge cake. Robert and Jane were carrying it between them.

'Phew – this weighs a ton!' Robert said. 'Let's find somewhere to put it down.'

The meadow beyond the playing field was dotted with family groups setting out their picnics. Anthea, carrying the rug, ran ahead to bag an excellent spot in the dappled shade of a willow tree. Edie's spirits soared; the loveliest thing about being all together again was that it felt so normal – as if the whole war had been a dream. The Bigguns stopped behaving like worried grown-ups and became themselves again, joking and shoving and giggling. Jane poured them all glasses of Mrs Field's delicious lemonade, cloudy and sweet.

'This is bliss!' Anthea sighed. 'Music and sunshine – after such a beastly wet winter.'

'I invited Harper's sister,' Cyril said, 'but she had to go home. I wanted you all to meet her – it'll have to wait till next time now.'

'Look here,' Robert said, 'that's about the thousandth time you've dragged Miss Harper's name into a completely unrelated conversation. I think she must be rather pretty.'

'Shut up!' Cyril flicked lemonade at him. 'She's extremely pretty, but it's none of your business.'

'Does she look like Harper?' Edie asked, and then remembered that Cyril didn't know she'd ever seen him. The Lamb shot her a scowl.

'She does and she doesn't,' Cyril said with a slow, inward-looking smile. 'Her nose and mouth are just the same as his, but her eyes—'

'Oh, those HEAVENLY eyes!' Robert squeaked.

'I said shut up!'

'What-ho, Pembertons!' Lilian Winterbottom bounded across the grass towards them, her big hat all to one side. 'Crikey – the whole boiling lot of you!' She pumped the hands of all the girls and slapped the backs of the boys. 'Isn't it splendiferous that we're all on leave at the same time? The word at my depot is that it's because they're cranking up for a Big Push.'

'I hope you have time for another outing to the theatre, old bean,' Robert said. 'Father says he can get us very decent seats for *Tonight's the Night*.'

'Thanks Bobs – I'm here till Sunday week and I'll accept any outing most gratefully. Mother's being an utter barnacle, due to the fact that I've signed up to drive my ambulance in France. I've had enough of driving in London, and I'm sure I'd be more use nearer the front line.'

'Good for you!' Anthea was still rubbing her knuckles after Lilian's crushing handshake. 'The talk at my hospital's just the same. It's very quiet at the moment, but we all know there's something on the horizon. They've squashed two new huts into the grounds, and all the patients who are well enough have been sent home to make more space. It doesn't take a genius to work out that they're expecting an awful lot of casualties.'

'Girls, girls!' Cyril said. 'Stop worrying your pretty little heads about the war!'

'Oh, shut up,' Lilian said. 'Wait till I've thrashed you at tennis a couple of times – come over tomorrow and we'll make a party of it, as in the olden days of yore.'

'Gosh, I can't remember the last time we had a tennis party at Windytops,' Cyril said. 'My game's a bit rusty – we don't get much tennis on the Western Front – but I can still give you a run for your money.'

'Ha! You and whose army?'

The Bigguns moved off towards the tea tent in a laughing group around Lilian. The Lamb and Edie were left under the willow tree, lazily sipping warm lemonade and listening to the band as they waited for Mother and Father.

The Lamb fanned himself with his hat. 'I can't move. Sling us over some more lemonade.'

'Righto.' Too warm and contented to argue, Edie

opened the picnic basket – and let out a little yelp of shock when she saw the lump of brown fur curled up inside it. 'The Psammead! What's he doing here?'

The Lamb sat up straight. 'Well, he can't stay. Give him a prod to wake him up.'

Edie didn't like waking the Psammead, and gave him a timid prod with one finger. This was usually enough, but today the sand fairy only sighed and shifted to a more comfortable position on top of the cake tin.

'Here, I'll do it properly.' The Lamb grabbed a teaspoon and stuck it rudely into the Psammead's round stomach. 'I say, rise and shine!'

The sand fairy coughed and groaned. 'Is this the path before me?' he mumbled.

'He's dreaming.' Edie dared to shake his skinny shoulder, but he shrugged her hand off crossly and went back to sleep.

'Oh, lor,' the Lamb said. 'What on earth do we do if we can't get rid of him?' He stared at the slumbering Psammead, trying to think. 'I'll run for the Bigguns.'

'No!' Edie grabbed his sleeve. 'Don't you dare leave me alone! He might be ill. And what if the parents get back first?'

'Keep your hair on. I'll pick him up and give him a jolly good shake.'

'NO!'

'All right! What if I hide him under my blazer?'

'I suppose that would be better than leaving him in the basket – I'll do it!' Edie didn't trust the Lamb not to shake the Psammead, as he'd so heartlessly suggested. Very gently she lifted him out of the picnic basket. Normally the smallest touch woke him up at once. Today his long arms and legs dangled limply and a light snore whistled through his furry lips. Edie put him down beside the trunk of the willow tree and carefully spread the Lamb's blazer on top of him.

'That ought to do it,' the Lamb said. 'We can easily keep an eye on him if we sit nearby.'

The Gondoliers finished, to a scattering of applause. A moment later the band began to play 'There's a Long, Long Trail A-Winding'.

'This is Mabel Harper's favourite song,' Edie said. 'Cyril told me he paid the band at the Kardomah tea room to play it for her. Wasn't that romantic? I wonder if they'll get married.'

'Yeuch,' the Lamb said scornfully. 'You're always marrying people off.'

'I'm practically the only girl in my class who's never been a bridesmaid, that's all. And it's no use waiting for Panther and Ernie, when we're not even allowed to say they're engaged, or at least not until he's got enough money to marry her.'

'Well, I wish you'd give it a rest. Just because Cyril's taken a girl out a couple of times—'

'Shh! What's that?'

'What's what?'

There was a low, mumbling, humming sound – and it was coming from underneath the Lamb's blazer. They both bent over it.

'Crikey,' the Lamb said, 'he's – singing!'

They had never heard the Psammead singing before; his voice was sandy and musty and not tuneful, but the words were clear:

> *'There's a long, long trail a-winding*
> *Into the land of my dreams,*
> *Where the nightingales are singing*
> *And a white moon beams.'*

'I didn't know he knew any songs – let alone a modern one,' Edie said.

The blazer twitched and moved. Edie gasped and made a dive for it – but not in time to stop the Psammead from suddenly scuttling away from them through the long dry grass.

The Lamb and Edie watched, frozen with shock, as the small brown figure – looking very strange indeed – moved determinedly away from them towards the next group of people. The sand fairy didn't move very often or very far, but he was now propelling his squat body with his long arms and legs like an enormous spider, and he could move surprisingly quickly.

'Come on – before anyone sees him.' The Lamb scrambled to his feet and dashed after him. Edie followed, so appalled by the sight of her beloved Psammead running away that she forgot to be careful about her new silk dress and accidentally put her foot through the hem.

A few yards away a grandly dressed pair of ladies on folding picnic chairs were sipping tea. To the huge relief of Edie and the Lamb they didn't move a hair when the Psammead ran over their feet.

'They can't see him,' panted the Lamb.

'He must be sleepwalking!' Edie gasped. 'He's never done this before.'

The Psammead was invisible but they were not. A couple of people looked cross as the two dishevelled children pelted across the meadow towards a small cluster of trees. Edie didn't care; it turned her cold to think of the Psammead waking up without her and calling for her in vain.

They chased him into the wood, and out again into a stubbly hayfield belonging to the farm next to the school. For a moment they thought they'd lost him, until the Lamb breathlessly pointed to a brown figure vanishing through a gap in the hedge and they dashed after him.

There was another field on the other side of the hedge. The Psammead suddenly slowed down, and the Lamb and Edie were able to catch up with him.

'I don't believe it – he's still asleep,' the Lamb said. 'He's moving but his eyes are folded in and he's snoring!'

Their faces were scarlet and shiny with sweat. Edie looked at her hands; she'd fallen over a couple of times and her palms were dirty but perfectly dry – the sun had baked the mud to dust. As soon as she got her breath back, she bent down to pick up the Psammead.

'What? Hmm?' His telescope eyes drooped with sleep. 'Where am I? Put me back in my sand!'

'I'd love to, but your sand bath's not here,' the Lamb said. 'You chose to make one of your surprise appearances at the sports-day picnic.'

'Picnic?'

'I can't hear the band,' Edie said suddenly. 'And something's different – I don't think this is the same field we were in a minute ago.'

They looked around; this was definitely a different field. A long, straight road ran beside the field, lined with tall trees. There was a tramp-tramp-tramp sound of dozens of pairs of boots coming along the road. Through a gap in the hedge they saw soldiers marching past with heavy packs on their backs.

'My hat, he's done it again!' the Lamb said. 'We've been snatched away right from under our own noses!'

'Where are we?'

'Not in Kent, that's for sure.'

As if to underline this, a tremendous explosion nearly knocked them off their feet.

'Stop squeezing me,' the Psammead said. 'I was having such an agreeable dream, until you two ruined it.'

'We did not!' The Lamb was indignant. 'This is nothing to do with us – you just turned up in our basket!'

'If I did, I suppose there must have been a reason,' the Psammead said. 'Perhaps you have been called as witnesses. All right, I'll let you tag along, provided you keep quiet.'

'I don't think we have any choice,' Edie said. 'Do you know where we are?'

'It's obviously a bit of the Western Front. Put me down, please.'

'You won't leave without us, will you?'

'Of course not – put me down!'

Reluctantly, Edie placed the sand fairy on the ground. He immediately hurried away from them to join the column of marching soldiers on the road. The small, brown creature shuffled along calmly, dodging the heavy boots. The Lamb and Edie followed him, hemmed in by the hot, grimy, silent men. When they came to a crossroads the Psammead dropped out of the marching column, and the soldiers (who couldn't see or hear them) tramped on towards the sound of gunfire.

'There's something I have to look at,' the Psammead

said. 'Come along – I haven't a clue where we're going, but on this journey there's only one possible way to go.'

The two children gave each other helpless looks; this was the most unsettling place the Psammead had so far taken them, because it was the strangest – they were definitely here, but at one remove from reality, as if watching through glass.

'I hope we get back to the picnic soon.' Edie thought wistfully of the band, sunshine, music, cake.

It was a very long journey; the Lamb said later that it seemed to last for days. They walked and walked without getting tired, as if moving weightlessly through a dream. And most of it was horrible beyond anything they could have imagined – but they watched it in the same distant way that they watched silent, black-and-white films at the cinema.

They walked through landscapes that were nothing but vast oceans of black mud, where bombs sent up great fountains of earth. They walked past charred ruins and dead horses. Sometimes the sun shone, sometimes it rained, and the sky changed from blue to white to grey, always flashing and flickering with gunfire. They walked through wastelands of rusted barbed wire.

And the strangest thing of all was that they kept coming across the same line of marching soldiers – sometimes just glimpsed from the end of a trench, sometimes right in the middle of them. And everywhere they went more and more soldiers came to join them, until the line stretched as far as the eye could see. The Psammead would walk with the soldiers for a while, and then hop away on a detour, only to rejoin them.

They weren't moving through real time or space; this was obvious when the Psammead suddenly turned a corner and they found themselves on a crowded London street. Before they had time to clear their heads he was walking away from them into a fashionable tea shop, where officers and ladies were eating cakes and sandwiches.

'Cyril!' Edie cried out. 'But what's he doing here? Why isn't he at sports day?'

At a small table in the quietest corner Cyril sat with a girl in a grey dress. They were holding hands.

'Oh, lor,' the Lamb groaned softly. 'Isn't this awful enough without another love scene?'

Edie moved closer. The girl had a sweet, fair face, thick brown hair and pretty blue eyes. 'This must be

Mabel – oh, I do wish I could meet her properly! She looks just like Harper.'

'I'll wait outside, thanks.' The Lamb turned round and tried to walk out of the tea shop, but it kept swinging him back to where he'd started.

'It's no use,' Edie said. 'It's just like when we saw Anthea and Ernie. You might as well give in.'

'But it's so amazingly embarrassing—'

'Shut up, I think it's lovely.'

'It's always rotten to go back,' Cyril was saying. 'This time it's going to be a hundred times worse because of meeting you. I've never really allowed myself to think about the future. There didn't seem any point while the war's on. Now I find that I want one – a future, that is.'

'We have to hope for it,' Mabel said. 'There has to be something left to hope for. It really can't last forever, and then everybody will have to think of something else to do.'

'I can't imagine what I'll do after the war. When I was a kid, I wanted to be a famous explorer and have a waterfall named after me.' Cyril smiled and squeezed her hand. 'But this war's a much bigger adventure.'

And then Edie and the Lamb were suddenly back

on the busy street, following the Psammead through a crowd of well-dressed people – who gradually changed into the column of marching soldiers.

'I'm glad that's over,' the Lamb said. 'Let's never tell Cyril we saw him being romantic – it'd make him sick as a cat.'

'Oh, stop going on about it,' Edie said. 'You'll fall in love yourself one day.'

'I will not! And don't you dare let Winterbum hear you saying stuff like that.'

They were on a country road now. The Psammead moved away to a nearby hedge – and when they followed him through the hedge they were suddenly lashed with a wet, freezing gust of wind and found themselves bumping and sliding down the sides of a gigantic hole in an ocean of black mud. At the bottom of the hole, in two feet of brown water, a small group of soldiers huddled together while machine guns hammered and bombs screeched around them.

'We're in a shell hole – a huge one – and someone's big guns are going like crazy – but none of it can hurt us,' the Lamb said stoutly. 'We mustn't be scared.'

'Aren't you scared?'

'No – yes—'

'Where's the Psammead?'

It was hard to see anything clearly in the gloom of the muddy shell hole, until they heard a loud hissing noise above them, like a rocket on bonfire night, and for a few seconds the whole landscape was bathed in lurid, dazzling light, and Edie saw the Psammead squatting on the shoulder of one of the soldiers.

'It's Cyril – but we just left him in a tea shop!' The Lamb had to shout above the noise. He and Edie clung to each other; they were both terrified to see him in the middle of such danger, with the shells crashing around them, sometimes so close that black soil rained down on their heads.

'We'll wait here till dark,' Cyril told the other soldiers, 'and try to make a dash for it when the barrage lets up – everyone all right?'

'Yes, sir,' the other men said.

'Who's here?'

'Benson, Robbins, Fleetwood and the two Smiths, sir,' one of the men said.

'Good-oh,' Cyril said. 'Did anyone see what happened to the others?'

They all shook their heads.

'I've got a tin of toffees and it still seems quite dry. Let's all have one now to keep us going,' Cyril said.

And then they were walking behind the Psammead again, along a narrow, leafy lane, and there was Cyril, without his helmet and raincoat, looking perfectly brisk and cheerful.

'So what we saw just now must be something that happened in the past,' Edie said. There was no gunfire now. They were in a very ordinary green field, and though they were surrounded by soldiers, none of them were carrying rifles; they seemed relaxed and unhurried, strolling in twos and threes. 'Perhaps this is the end of the war.'

'Keep up!' the Psammead called over his shoulder. 'I think we're nearly there!'

'Nearly where?' the Lamb asked. 'Isn't it time to go home yet?'

'Through the gate, that's where everybody's going.'

Edie was about to say there was no gate, and nobody seemed to be going anywhere, when the Psammead scuttled through a tall wooden gate set in a thick hedge. The Lamb and Edie ran through it after him, and found themselves in a landscape of gentle green hills. Though the Psammead had said 'everybody' was going there, it was deserted.

'At last!' The Psammead let out a deep sigh and collapsed in a snoring heap on the grass.

The two children stood staring down at him, wondering what they were meant to do next. Everything was very quiet, and looming in front of them was a grand stone arch with writing carved into it.

The Lamb read the words out loud: 'NOW HEAVEN IS BY THE YOUNG INVADED.'

'I don't like this place,' Edie murmured. 'It looks like the green meadow the Psammead's always on about, but the white flowers aren't white flowers at all, they're crosses – thousands of white crosses.'

Nineteen

RAGTIME

THE GROUND BENEATH THEIR feet was firm again, and they were back in the field next to the Lamb's school. They could hear the brass band, blackbirds quarrelling in a nearby tree, and the summery sounds of sports day and the picnic.

The Psammead was curled around one of Edie's dusty feet. He sat up suddenly. 'Ugh! What am I doing here?'

And then he vanished.

Pale and shaking, Edie and the Lamb let out long, long sighs of relief.

'Don't take this the wrong way,' the Lamb said, 'but I was never so glad to see the back of anyone in my entire life – remind me not to get caught up in one of his crackpot dreams again.'

'It was just a dream, wasn't it?' Edie shook her head to clear away the fogginess.

'Of course it was – or we wouldn't have seen Squirrel, would we?'

'Did we really? The pictures in my mind are turning sort of – misty.'

'Mine too.'

'I can't quite remember – what did we see?'

'I'm not sure, the pieces are breaking up.'

'My dress!' Edie's head had cleared enough to see the great rip in her skirt; the white silk was grey with dust and there was a large hole in one of her stockings.

'Oh, lor,' the Lamb said, smiling grimly, 'I've just noticed what we look like – we're a couple of scarecrows!'

His white shirt and trousers were grubby and grass-stained. Their hands and faces were covered with smears and smudges.

'We can't go back to the picnic like this!' Edie moaned. 'Mother will have fifty fits!'

'Here,' the Lamb said and fished his handkerchief out of his pocket. 'It's not clean, but it's not as dirty as the rest of me.'

They tried to wipe off the worst of the dirt, but one grubby handkerchief didn't make much difference.

'Nothing else for it,' the Lamb said. 'It looks like you and I are about to face some pretty stiff music – and it won't be the *Gondoliers*.'

★

'We all did our best to stick up for you,' Jane said later, when they were back at the house, and gathered in Anthea's bedroom. 'We guessed it was Psammead-related. Sorry you had to get into hot water.'

The hot water was considerable. Mother was very cross, and very shocked that they'd managed to get so dirty in such a short time, and almost insisted on taking them home early. Luckily, Father thought it was funny and gave them his big handkerchief soaked with water to clean their faces properly.

'Don't worry about the dress, anyway,' Anthea said. 'I can easily repair it, and that white silk washes nicely.'

'That's all very well,' the Lamb said gloomily. 'We've both been fined a month's pocket money. It's all right for Edie because she's just had a birthday, but I'm penniless.'

'I'll make that up to you,' Cyril said.

'Good stuff!' The Lamb's mood immediately lifted and he took a bite from the slice of cake Jane had brought upstairs.

'For the last time,' the Psammead said, 'I did NOT attend your picnic, nor did I hitch a ride in your basket.' He was sitting on Anthea's bed, radiating dignity. 'As far as I'm concerned, I was simply having a beautiful dream.'

'Beautiful?' Edie cried. 'Most of it was horrid!'

'Which bits?'

'I don't know – the mud – the explosions—'

'The entire thing was clearly some sort of shared hallucination,' Robert said. 'You can't really have seen old Squirrel – back in the real world he was in the tea tent.'

'Now heaven is by the young invaded,' Cyril said quietly, repeating the words that the Lamb and Edie had read on the stone arch. 'Well, that's true enough. Old people don't seem to be dying anymore – and young people don't seem to be doing anything else.'

They were all silent.

'That was the rotten thing about today,' Robert said, 'finding out how many of the boys have gone west.

And the masters too – Monsieur Durand bought it at
Verdun. Remember how we used to rag him during
French lessons?'

'Lord, yes,' Cyril said. 'Poor old thing, he wasn't
such a bad oeuf.'

'I took that writing on the arch as an awful warning,'
the Psammead sniffed. 'I'm not sure I want to go to
heaven if it's been invaded by the young and it's all
bad manners and RAGTIME music.'

This was so amazingly heartless that they all burst
out laughing.

'Good old Psammead!' Cyril said.

'Tell you what,' Robert said, 'let's have some ragtime
right now – the parents and servants are out, and if
we bring the Psammead downstairs he can wind up
the gramophone and change the records.'

'Oh, all right,' the Psammead said. 'I'll perform
that menial task just this once, to honour the fact
that you're all together again.' He was trying to sound
cross, but his furry lips twitched happily; the ancient
sand fairy secretly loved working the gramophone,
even if he didn't approve of the music they played
on it.

Edie stopped worrying about her muddled memories

251

of the dream journey; reality was a lot more fun. The six of them ran downstairs laughing and shoving; Cyril slid down the banisters, magnificent in his uniform. They all helped push back the furniture and roll up the rugs to clear the sitting-room floor for dancing. The Psammead took his place beside the shining wooden gramophone, and they laughed even harder at the scornful way he read out the names of the records.

'"Shaking the Shimmy", "K-K-K-Katy", "Ragging the Baby to Sleep" – really, your music mystifies me! And as for the words – I just wish I could speak to my court poet, poor Mapeth.'

'You wished,' Edie said. 'Does that mean we're going to see Mapeth now?'

'No,' the Psammead snapped. 'I don't decide the wishes anymore.'

'Put on "Shaking the Shimmy",' Cyril said. 'Jane, help me to brush up my two-step.'

It was very entertaining to see the Psammead putting the record on the turntable with his little paws, and winding the handle of the gramophone. Cyril danced with Jane, Robert danced with Edie, and Anthea danced with the Lamb (he refused to dance with anyone else). Cyril opened the French windows, and they danced through every record in the collection until the garden was grey-blue with dusk.

'I like this machine,' the Psammead said. 'In my days as a desert god, I tried to shrink my palace orchestra to a tiny size – I wanted to put them in a box, so I could take them to picnics. But this invention is far more convenient.'

When it was properly dark and they were all breathless, Jane went to the kitchen to fetch lemonade. Then Anthea played 'There's a Long, Long Trail' on the piano so that everyone could hear the Psammead singing. The solemn look on his face was so funny that they all (except devoted Edie) struggled not to offend him by laughing.

For the last chorus they all joined in:

There's a long, long trail a-winding
Into the land of my dreams,
Where the nightingales are singing
And a white moon beams.
There's a long, long night of waiting
Until my dreams all come true,
Till the day when I'll be winding
Down that long, long trail with you.

When they heard the pony-trap in the lane, bringing their parents home, Edie carried the Psammead up to the attic.

He yawned and wriggled down in his soft sand. 'What a day!'

'Did you learn anything from the universe this time?' Edie asked.

'Hmmm, let me think.' The Psammead yawned again. 'There is something. That writing on the stone arch reminded me how hard – how very hard – wars are for the young. The old people only start them.'

He sank deeper into the sand and disappeared.

Twenty

TELEGRAMS

ON A BEAUTIFUL, STILL JULY morning, a few weeks
after Anthea and the boys had gone, Mrs Trent
from the post office rode her creaking old bicycle
along the lane to the White House. She was bringing
a telegram, and that was a dreadful thing these days;
the girls at school who had lost their fathers whispered
about the moment their worlds had ended when the
telegram arrived. Lizzie the maid carried it into the
dining room as if holding a bomb.

They were in the middle of breakfast; Edie and the
Lamb were bickering mildly about the last half-inch of
strawberry jam. The sight of the small brown envelope
silenced them at once. For a few seconds there was a
breathless quiet, like the moment when a glass teeters
on the edge of a shelf before falling off and shattering.

Father took the envelope, ripped it open, and seemed to shrink.

'Who?' Mother cried out.

Father got up and put his arms around her; that was when Edie, Jane and the Lamb knew this was the news they had been dreading.

'It's Bobs,' he said. 'Killed in action.'

Mother let out a cry like a wounded animal.

And suddenly everything in the world was wrong.

Nobody went to school and Father stayed away from his office. He took Mother upstairs to their bedroom. Mrs Field, wiping her eyes, pulled down all the blinds, giving the house an underwater gloom. There was nothing to be done, but everyone seemed to be hanging about, waiting for something to do.

'I want dreadfully to see the Psammead,' Edie said, 'but I've cried so much that he'll only get cross.'

'We should tell him as soon as we can,' Jane said. 'Just like they say you're meant to tell things to bees – births and deaths – in case they swarm.'

'Let's wait for Panther,' the Lamb said.

Anthea had sent a telegram saying that she was on her way home. She arrived late in the afternoon and everyone in the house was glad to see her. Though her eyes were red from crying, she was calm and kind, and seemed to drive away everything that was strange and frightening. She kissed Mrs Field and Lizzie, and took a cup of beef tea up to Mother and a glass of whisky to Father at his desk.

Later, when the still, hot dusk gathered over the garden and the fields beyond, Anthea came to the old nursery, where the others were waiting for her. For a long time they simply clung together. As the last gleam of sunset vanished, Jane lit the lamp and two fat moths immediately began to hurl themselves at the glass shade.

'Dear old Bobs,' Anthea said. 'I can't quite make myself believe it. A couple of weeks ago he was right here, throwing paper darts at my hair. How can he be gone if I can see him so clearly?'

'We haven't told the Psammead yet.' Edie leaned against Anthea. 'I just couldn't bear to – saying it aloud makes it feel more real.'

'He'll be as glad as the rest of us to see Panther,' Jane said. 'Let's tell him now.' She scrubbed her face with her sleeve.

'I'm the driest,' the Lamb said sternly. He was stern because he'd spent the whole day trying to cry as little as possible; his heart was broken, but only girls cried. 'I'll go and get him.'

By the tiny flame of Edie's night light, he went up to the attic and dug the Psammead out of his sand bath.

'What? What's going on?'

'Wake up. This is an emergency.'

The Psammead's telescope eyes came out properly. 'Ugh, leave me alone. The air's all soggy and painful with TEARS – the ends of my whiskers are AGONY!'

But he allowed the Lamb to carry him down to the old nursery. 'Anthea! Why didn't you tell me she was coming home?' His eyes sharply scanned their faces. 'Something has happened.'

Anthea told him about Robert.

There was a long silence, and Edie furtively went behind the bookcase to wipe her eyes.

'But I don't understand this,' the Psammead said, 'the universe was supposed to take ME first!' A violent shudder ran through his furry body. 'Lamb, please put me back in my bath – your tears are on the inside, but they hurt as much as anyone else's – ow – OW! The TORMENT!'

'Selfish little beast,' the Lamb said furiously. 'Is this

the best you can do, when our brother's dead?'

'Dead?' The Psammead was surprised. 'But Robert's not dead! Don't you see? Mapeth was only lost, and the universe reminded me about him for a reason – he was found by his true love, the warrior maiden. Now kindly stop crying and LEAVE ME ALONE!' He pulled in his eyes and hugged his limbs to his body.

Anthea took him back to his sand bath.

'I'm not touching him again,' the Lamb said through gritted teeth, 'in case I get carried away and wring his disgusting little neck!'

Five days after that first, dreadful telegram, another one came. When Father read it, he let out a great shout and shoved it joyously at Mother.

This telegram said:

ROBERT ALIVE BUT BADLY WOUNDED STOP
LETTER FOLLOWS STOP LILIAN
WINTERBOTTOM

Twenty-one

WARRIOR MAIDEN

Letter from Lilian Winterbottom, Ambulance Depot,
Etaples, to Anthea Pemberton, July 1916

My dear old Ant,

I've written to your people but this letter is just for you; I can tell you the whole story because you've seen the same awful things as me, and you'll be able to prepare them for the shock when Robert comes home. The poor old boy was hit by a fragment of shell on the first day of the Big Push on the Somme. His left cheekbone, eye socket and left eye were blown away. His other eye is still there but quite blind. The doctor told me his optic nerve has gone and he'll never see again; they're still waiting to see if there was any damage to his brain. He's alive and that's the main thing – but they mustn't expect the same old Bobs.

I'm still reeling from the walloping luck of finding him. I'd just had Mother's letter about Bobs being killed, and it made me so low that I nearly bunked off work for the day. But I couldn't when we're so frantic – trainloads of wounded are coming in faster than we can get them to the hospital.

Oh, Anthea, it's so terrible. I'm not surprised that Bobs got declared dead by mistake when everything here is chaos. The clearing stations at the front don't have enough time or space to assess the wounded; they just bundle them all – British, French, German – onto the nearest hospital train, and many are dying or dead by the time they reach my ambulance. My job is to take them to one of the vast hospital encampments here at Etaples.

The dead ones go to the morgue (a grand name for a group of shabby tents) and the ones who are at the point of death go to one of the huts set aside for the 'moribund'. Truthfully, they are the places I hate most in the camp. It would break your heart to see these boys moments from dying, with no familiar faces around them.

Anyway, I found Bobs when I delivered a patient to the moribund hut. I saw the name 'Pemberton' chalked on one of the little blackboards they have at the foot of each

261

bed. And despite the fact that his head was covered with dressings and bandages, I knew my old pal at once. I'm afraid I forgot everything else for a moment. I ran to take his hand and started babbling at him in my usual madcap fashion (you'll remember how I was always being sent out for chattering when we were at school). I simply refused to believe he couldn't hear me and kept telling him over and over that I was there.

Then all of a sudden there was an officer looming over me – wearing a dog collar with his uniform, so I knew it was the chaplain. His name is Mr Ince and he's a jolly good sort when you get to know him. He was frosty at first – I had to explain that I'd known Bobs for years, and he'd been declared dead.

He said, 'All the same, you don't belong in here.'

'No,' I said, 'and neither does Lieutenant Pemberton! I'm not budging until he gets moved to a proper ward, because he's not dying if I have anything to do with it!'

Mr Ince saw I was serious and fetched a ward sister.

She said, 'I'm very sorry, but we're desperately short of space and the other wards are for men who will live.'

'He's going to live,' I said. 'And I'm sticking right beside him.'

The ward sister pursed up her mouth and fetched a tired-looking doctor.

Tired as he was, he took a long and careful look at Bobs.

'There's no infection,' he said. 'No swelling of the brain and no fever – he might just have a chance.'

And he moved Bobs to a proper ward for the living, where he'll have the very best care – I could've whooped and turned a cartwheel. I stayed with him until I'd seen him settled, then scooted back to the ambulance depot. Good old Mr Ince arranged to send my telegram to your parents, but I was in an ocean of hot water for deserting my post in the middle of a shift.

The moment I was free I borrowed a bike and went straight back to Bobs (which is amazingly against the rules but I don't care). There are nineteen other men in his hut, all French. One of the VADs told me it made her wish she'd paid more attention at school; fortunately the other VAD had a French governess and does most of the translating.

The ward sister didn't like me hanging around at first but

I've worked hard at not getting in the way, and even lend a hand where I can – like everyone else, they're run off their feet. And I make it perfectly clear to all and sundry that if they want me to leave they'll need to find at least six able-bodied men to carry me out!

Truthfully, Bobs is not out of the woods yet. But I know he's getting better. I sat up with him all last night and had my reward this morning when he squeezed my hand and said, 'Hello, old bean.'

Joy and rapture! I could have cheered – but I surprised myself by starting to cry instead, and had to make sure my weedy tears didn't fall where he could feel them.

Where there's life there's hope, as my mother would say, and for once I agree with her.

I'll write again the minute there's any change.

Chin up,

Lilian

'HURRAH FOR OLD AIRY-FAIRY,' Father said, with tears running down his cheeks. 'Henceforth the name of Winterbum shall be held sacred in this house.'

'That dear, good girl. She's saved my boy's life,' Mother said.

After the horror of thinking they had lost him, knowing that Robert was alive was wonderful, like getting the greatest present in the world. The Lamb ripped off his black armband and (much to the annoyance of Mrs Field) threw it on the kitchen fire, where it burned with an awful stench.

'I don't want to sound smug,' the Psammead said, with the utmost smugness, 'but I told you so.'

Lilian's letters from the hospital rained down at the rate of two or three a week. She spent every spare moment beside Robert, and reported every single hopeful change. The changes happened very slowly, but as the terrible summer of 1916 began to mellow into autumn, he got strong enough to send them messages, and was moved to another hospital further behind the lines. Lilian – to Mother's delight – managed to get transferred to another unit, so that she could stay beside him.

265

'I can't recall the name of Mapeth's warrior maiden,' the Psammead said. 'She was a big, strapping, healthy sort of girl – and she gave me a mighty telling-off for sending him to war in the first place.'

'That was brave of her,' Jane said, 'considering the sort of things you did to anyone who disagreed with you.'

'To tell the truth, I was genuinely sorry,' the Psammead said. 'I gave the two of them a very convenient little house beside the palace rubbish pit because I felt I owed them something. The universe teaches me that when people make sacrifices for their leaders, they deserve a little something in return.'

'Gosh, that's pretty much Father's editorial in the latest *Citizen*,' Jane said. 'He says we can't let our fighting men return to lives of poverty. They should have jobs that pay decent wages, and houses that aren't slums. You must be turning into a socialist.'

'Steady on,' the Lamb said. 'It was only a house beside a beastly rubbish pit.'

The Psammead drew himself up haughtily. 'It was bright and airy – and a lot better than Mapeth's old room in the palace. He was thrilled, and wrote a lovely song about my generosity.'

'Because you told him to.'

'Because the warrior maiden told him to,' the Psammead said. 'And she wasn't the sort of girl you disobeyed.'

Twenty-two

A FORMAL INTRODUCTION

IN OCTOBER, CYRIL CAME HOME AGAIN. He was on sick leave after his left arm had been badly broken when a dugout collapsed on top of him.

'I hate to say it was a piece of good luck,' he told the others, 'but the shameful fact is that we all pray for this sort of injury – just bad enough to get you sent home to mother, but without utterly wrecking you. The chaps call it "copping a Blighty". My arm has brought me a jolly nice little holiday – it's stupendous that I'll be here to welcome good old Bobs.'

A postcard had come that morning, written by Lilian and signed at the bottom with a shaky letter 'R', announcing Robert's homecoming the following afternoon. The next day the White House was in an uproar of excitement from early morning, and even though no one mentioned it, everyone was nervous about how Robert would look; he was blind, and Lilian had written that he was badly scarred. It was impossible to imagine.

'I keep catching myself making plans for him,' Cyril confessed. 'Fishing trips and cycling, that sort of thing. As if everything was back to normal. And, of course, it won't be. I think I'd go crazy if I couldn't read.'

'I'll read aloud to him as much as he likes,' Jane said. 'And Father wants him to learn Braille.' She added, to the Psammead, 'That's the method of reading for blind people – the words are raised dots they feel with their fingertips.'

'Hmm, very clever,' the Psammead said. 'Like the gramophone, another example of how you humans get round your shortage of magic.'

All the children had come up to the attic to wait for Robert, away from their agitated parents.

'It's science,' the Lamb said, 'which is the human version of magic – and a lot more reliable.'

'I wish Panther could be here,' Edie said, for the umpteenth time.

'She couldn't leave her hospital,' Jane said. 'Half

the other nurses have come down with influenza, and they're rushed off their feet. And she says it's awkward to be here when she hasn't told Mother and Father about Ernie – though I'm sure Mother's pretty much guessed there's something going on.'

The sand fairy's soft ears stiffened. 'Your brother is coming. Please bring him to me as quickly as you can – I can't settle properly until I've seen him.' He vanished into his sand.

A moment later they heard the village taxi sputtering along the lane.

'Bobs,' Edie murmured. Now that the moment had come, she was almost scared of seeing him again, in case he'd changed too much.

They all ran downstairs. The front door stood open and Mother was outside, with her arms around a tall, spindly figure in a baggy khaki uniform, laughing and crying at the same time. Father hugged him, and then the taxi drove away, leaving a heap of luggage and one other person – a beaming young woman in a tweed coat and skirt and a lopsided felt hat.

'Lilian!' Mother kissed her. 'Oh, my dear, we'll never be able to thank you enough!'

'You can thank me with a cup of tea and a slice of

Mrs Field's cake,' Lilian said, 'if such lovely things still exist.' She gently took Robert's arm. 'Two steps up, old bean.'

Slowly, uncertainly, Robert walked back into his home. For one still moment, the others stared at him in silence. The first sight was a shock; he looked as if someone had taken a bite out of his head. What had been his left eye was now a huge, puckered scar that dragged one side of his face out of shape.

But then he said, 'Hello,' and smiled in his old way, and they saw that he hadn't really changed at all. 'It's stupendous to be home – gosh, it smells so good after all those hospitals.'

That was all it took to stop the strangeness; he was immediately smothered by brothers and sisters, hugging him, shaking his hand, slapping his shoulder.

'Squirrel, is that you?'

'Yes, it's the genuine me – I managed to wangle some sick leave.'

'Crikey, Lamb – have you grown again? And Edie, you feel like a giraffe!'

They all went into the sitting room for tea. Robert kept a tight hold of Lilian's arm, and let her guide him to the softest chair beside the fire. Edie had been afraid he would be sad, but he was calm and cheerful.

'You see, I'm borrowing Lilian's eyes,' he told them all, 'which is the next best thing to having my own.'

'I don't understand how you managed to stay together,' Mother said 'But I'm so glad you did.'

'Well, the fact is—' Lilian stopped, and her beaming face turned bright red.

Robert squeezed her hand, laughing softly. 'The fact is – I hope you're sitting down, Mother – we got married.'

There was an electric silence, like the intake of breath before a giant clap of thunder. And then Mother let out a great squeak of joy and flung her egg-and-cress sandwich into the air; it landed on the Lamb's head, and the congratulations began with a burst of laughter. Father went to fetch the champagne he'd been saving for the end of the war, and came back with Mrs Field and Lizzie, so they could all toast the happy couple. Even Edie was allowed a small glass.

'Here's to Lilian,' Father said, 'my beautiful, brave new daughter – Bobs, old boy, make sure you deserve her.'

'I'll do my best,' Robert said.

Lilian's face was scarlet. 'I'm so sorry we had to do it like this – and I'm afraid my parents and Arthur are about to descend on you, since they'll have just got the rather mad telegram I sent them. It's all been such a rush, I don't know if I'm on my head or my heels.' She radiated happiness, and anyone could see that she was in love.

Edie knocked back her champagne too fast, and the sour fizz on her tongue made her want to sneeze. She liked Lilian, and she was thrilled by the romance of the sudden wedding, but what were they going to do about the Psammead? How could Robert visit him, if Lilian was always glued to his side?

They all sat down to have tea, and Lilian put plates and cups into Robert's hands as if she'd been doing it for years.

'Honestly, we would've told you if we'd time, but it all happened in a tearing hurry.' She held out her left hand to show them her wedding ring. 'For example, this came off a curtain.'

'You're wearing a curtain ring!' Mother was shocked.

'It's a perfect fit – though it has turned my finger

green.' Lilian smiled down at her brass wedding ring. 'I suppose I'll have to take it off eventually.'

'The hospital chaplain somehow found some flowers,' Robert said. 'My new wife whispered in my ear that they were orange rhododendrons and looked like mildewed mops – I really don't know what I'd do without her running commentary.'

'I do wish I'd been there!' Mother sighed. 'And I do wish you'd had a nicer wedding.'

Robert and Lilian squeezed each other's hands and laughed a private, lovers' laugh.

'It was a wonderful wedding,' Lilian said. 'I wouldn't change a single thing. We did it on the ward, the day before yesterday. The bride looked dazzling in her shabby Red Cross uniform. They wheeled in a jangly old piano, and one of the other patients played the wedding march.'

'And the very decent French chap in the next bed tore up his copy of *Le Figaro* to make confetti,' Robert said. 'He was my best man, too – and the ward sister acted as bridesmaid.'

'You see, I wanted to come home with Bobs, and nobody would let me.' Lilian put half a scone in Robert's hand. 'Jam ahoy, keep it rightside up.

Anyway, one of the doctors said it would be different if we were married – whereupon Bobs said, "What about it, old bean?"

'Not a very poetic proposal,' Robert said. 'I should've gone down on one knee.'

'For once, I was lost for words,' Lilian said. 'And then I saw that it was the perfect solution to absolutely everything. Because it turns out that I've loved the old boy all my life.'

★

The homecoming tea turned into a wedding party. Lilian's parents and brother arrived, and there were more tears and congratulations. Her mother was dismayed that Lilian had married a wounded man, but on the whole she was very relieved that she had married anybody at all.

'I wish you both all the joy in the world, dear. I'm only sorry we couldn't give you a proper wedding in a church.'

'Thank you for sparing me all that expense,' Lilian's father said.

'What are we going to do about the Psammead?'

Edie whispered to the Lamb. 'Lilian never leaves Bobs alone for a single second!'

'Oh, stop fussing about that sand fairy! There's plenty of time.' The Lamb was larking about with Winterbum over the fact that they were nearly brothers now, which was hilarious and also covered the embarrassment of all the wedding stuff. 'We'll get our chance to talk to Bobs when everyone's gone.'

'But how? I can't make a sign to him behind Lilian's back – he won't be able to see! We'll have to find a way of telling her.'

Edie needn't have worried. The first moment all the parents were out of the room, Lilian said, 'Quick, before they come back – when can I meet the Psammead?'

They all stared at her; it was so odd to hear her saying his name.

'Crikey,' Cyril said. 'You told her!'

'Naturally I told her,' Robert said. 'I can hardly keep a secret like that from my wife.'

'But – dearest Lilian, did you believe it?' Cyril was laughing softly. 'Weren't you the least bit suspicious that he was telling whoppers?'

Lilian's cheeks reddened. 'I must admit, it sounded

pretty far-fetched – but when he told me, I knew he wasn't lying, and he obviously hadn't lost his marbles.'

'My trusting old bean,' Robert said. 'When you see him, you'll have proof that my marbles are still a full set.'

'I know you'll like him.' Edie took Lilian's hand. 'You mustn't mind if he seems a bit rude at first.'

'You're his favourite, according to Bobs,' Lilian said, smiling. 'You must've been worried when I turned up – but you can trust me to keep quiet about your family secret, and I won't faint when I see him. I'm actually rather excited – I haven't a spark of imagination and things like this never happen to me normally.'

'I'll run up and fetch him after tea.' Edie's last doubt vanished and she gave Lilian a hug. 'I'm so glad you're here!'

After tea, when the guests had gone, Edie dug the Psammead out of his sand bath and carried him to the large spare room, where Mother had put the newly-weds. Robert sat in the armchair beside the fire, Lilian sat on the rug at his feet. When she saw the odd little creature settle himself on top of the coal bucket, her mouth dropped open and her eyes were saucers of amazement.

The Psammead's eyes shot out on their long stalks. He looked hard at Lilian.

'Bessa,' he said. 'That was her name! Bessa the Breaker, they called her, and she was a fine hand with a spear. This girl looks rather like her.'

The sound of his dusty little voice coming from his furry pucker of a mouth made Lilian gasp. 'Crikey!'

'Hello, Psammead,' Robert said, smiling. 'This is Lilian. I don't know what she's like with a spear, but she's pretty handy with everything else. She dragged me out of the jaws of death – and then she managed to convince me that I don't look like an utter monster.'

All the other children winced at this.

'You're not a monster,' Jane said. 'It was a bit of a shock at first, but now you just look like – you.'

'Honestly,' Cyril said shakily, 'you look absolutely fine – every bit as hideous as you've always been.'

Edie leaned over to touch Robert's arm. 'This might sound silly, but the biggest shock was seeing you without your glasses.'

Robert smiled. 'I don't need them nowadays. But I'll wear them if you like.'

'I think you look handsomer without them,' Edie said.

'I don't want to hear any more talk about monsters,'

the Psammead said briskly. 'I've seen plenty of monsters in my time, and you're nothing like any of them. As Jane rightly observes, you look more or less like your old self, only somewhat battered – like a statue that's been struck by lightning and then left outside in the rain for a few years.'

'Psammead!' Jane hissed.

She was afraid Robert would be hurt by this, but it made him laugh. 'Thanks, old boy.'

'And so this is Lilian.' The Psammead rolled his eyes over to her mesmerised face. 'How do you do.'

'H-h-how do—' she could hardly get the words out.

'My dear Robert, I congratulate you. Your wife looks like a nice girl.'

'The very nicest in the world,' Robert said. 'When I got hit I thought I'd had it. But Lilian wouldn't let me go.'

'Yes, her love for you is very strong. I give you both my blessing, for what it's worth these days. I've lost my ability to see clearly into the future, but I can tell you that you'll have a lot of very NOISY children.'

'Steady on!' Lilian squeaked and clapped her hands over her mouth. Everyone laughed quietly.

'Psammead, may I stroke you?' Robert said.

'You may – Lilian, kindly carry me to your husband.'

'Gosh – me? Really? I'd simply love to pick you up!' Very cautiously, Lilian leaned across the rug to pick up the Psammead, smiling when his paws clutched at her arm. 'Oh, AREN'T you a darling?'

Edie beamed at her. 'I knew you'd love him.'

'Psammead, old chap,' Cyril said, 'I wish I had your devastating way with girls.'

Trying to look stern and dignified, but with a gratified smirk lingering around his mouth, the Psammead settled himself royally on Robert's knee. Lilian guided Robert's hand to the sand fairy's back.

'Now I feel properly at home,' Robert said as he found the Psammead's head and began to stroke him. 'Gosh, this takes me back – we had some good old times, didn't we?'

The Psammead's whiskers quivered. 'The magic is upon me – it won't be much, as I can only perform minor conjuring tricks these days.' He puffed himself up to bursting point and held his breath. 'There.'

Edie was worried that they were all about to be whisked away somewhere crazy, and was relieved that nothing had changed. 'What did you do?'

'Lilian, my dear,' the Psammead said, 'look at your wedding ring.'

She held out her left hand, where her ring glinted richly in the firelight. 'It's different – what's happened to it?'

'Oh, it's nothing,' the Psammead said modestly. 'It's still a curtain ring, I'm afraid, but I wished I could change it to the same fine metal as your heart – and it turned to real Roman gold. I only wish I could give you something better.'

'It's perfect!' Lilian kissed the Psammead. 'Thank you – and thank you all, for making me feel so welcome. I've never been so happy in my life – I've got an A1 husband, a solid gold curtain ring – and a new name that isn't Winterbum!'

Twenty-three

WITNESSES AT A TRIBUNAL

1917

Letter from Captain C. Pemberton,
Flanders, to 'Sammy & Co', January 1917

Dear Bobs, Lilian, Jane, Lamb, Edie and 'Sammy',

A very happy New Year to all of you. As you can see, my promotion's come through. I'm now a Captain. I'm writing this in the picturesque setting of the officer's club in a small town close behind the lines, where I've just had a very decent lunch. It's the first free afternoon I've had since I came back. Most of my time recently has been spent penned up in a trench with my chaps – a tremendous bunch they are too. I wish the types who moan about the shortages at home could see the things my chaps endure without a word of complaint.

Most of them were called up and thrown straight into the fighting, and they come from all sorts of backgrounds – one of my best men used to play the accordion at a tea shop in Cheam. Another is a giant of a blacksmith, who's as brave as a lion, except that he's terrified of rats – his girlish shrieks make us all laugh. He wants to shoot the little blighters, but that's forbidden due to the shortage of bullets.

Actually, the rats are a constant nuisance. A sergeant in my company tried bringing a cat up the line to fight them off. But the cat was heavily outnumbered and after two nights it was a nervous wreck – a motorcycle runner took it back to HQ in disgrace. Round one to the rodents.

Sammy, we need a touch of your magic – could you send the Pied Piper of Hamelin? Or perhaps do something about the MUD? This is a horribly wet winter and absolutely everything is caked with the stuff, even the food.

This is the time of year for taking stock and I can hardly believe it's the third New Year of this endless war. It makes me think about the friends and comrades (especially good old Harper) I've lost since it all kicked off; so many that there's never enough time to remember them properly. I sometimes imagine I can hear them calling out to me, begging not to be forgotten.

People mustn't ever forget, or allow it to happen again.

God bless you all,

Cyril

'MY FOURTH YEAR HERE!' remarked the Psammead. 'This is the longest I've stayed anywhere since I got burned at the stake and went into hiding. And if anyone else says the war can't go on forever, I'll explode.'

It was a cold, dark, sloppy afternoon at the tail end of January. Edie had finished school and the Lamb had a half day. Still in their coats, they were huddled under a moth-eaten blanket on the musty old sofa in the attic.

'There was the Seven Years War,' the Lamb said, 'and the Hundred Years War. But I don't see how this war can last for seven years – the world will simply run out of people.'

'Lamb, you are gloomy today,' the Psammead said. 'Has something occurred at your school?'

'We had bad news, that's all. The chap who was head boy last year was killed in action, and we all liked him. Today would've been his nineteenth birthday.'

The Psammead sighed. 'More broken hearts – and for what? The sadness creeps into the air, until the entire landscape drips with it. I just WISH I could see something HAPPY come out of this wretched war!'

An invisible hand tore the blanket off the Lamb and Edie.

A half-second later it was broad daylight and they were floating on a soft breeze, above a noisy, teeming London street. Edie yelped and pulled her skirt over her knees.

'This is more like it!' The Lamb paddled his legs in the air. 'Flying at last – even if we didn't get the wings!' He turned a somersault. 'I was beginning to think all your wishes were damp squibs these days.'

Edie reached out for the Psammead, who was floating beside her with his limbs folded, like a furry brown cushion. The sight of the city spread out beneath them – with dozens of church spires piercing the grey sky – took her breath away. 'Where are we?'

'I know!' the Lamb shouted. 'That wide road with all the trams is Fleet Street – where the newspapers are printed. Father's office is near here.'

'We're losing height,' the Psammead said. 'Don't squeeze me, Edie – Lamb, kindly stop fooling about.'

'Not likely!' The Lamb was twisting and diving through the air. 'I'm having far too much fun!'

'You're not here to have fun. Come down at once.'

'Oh, go and boil your head – I'll come when I'm ready!'

'Don't you speak to him like that!' Edie aimed a furious swipe at the Lamb's leg as he flew past. 'And stop spoiling his lesson!'

'All right, keep your hair on.'

They were, as the Psammead had said, slowly losing height, and Fleet Street seemed to be rising up around them – crammed with trams, buses, motor cars and hansom cabs, and crowds of people hovering at every doorway. Men in leather aprons wheeled huge rolls of paper on trolleys.

Though it was a cold winter's day, the air around them was warm and pleasant, and gently tugging them towards something.

'It's like being a kite on a piece of string.' Edie had stopped worrying about people seeing up her skirt, and was starting to enjoy herself. 'Wouldn't they all be amazed if they COULD see us?'

They floated above the pavement and were suddenly sucked into a narrow alley lined with crooked, sooty, old houses, where they stopped just above the offices of the *New Citizen*.

'Good stuff, we can spy on Father,' the Lamb said, 'and then stagger him at dinner by telling him what he's been up to!'

Another puff of air wafted them down to the roof, where grubby-looking pigeons fluttered between the chimney pots. They dropped downwards, slowly enough for Edie to peer through the attic window and glimpse three small brown mice running in a circle on the dusty floor.

The cobbled pavement was closer now. They finally stopped several feet above it, outside a large and dirty pair of windows on the first floor. This was Father's office. He was standing beside the fireplace, talking to two people were sitting with their backs to the windows.

'It's Anthea and Ernie!' Edie cried. 'Oh, how nice!'

'I've a horrible feeling this is another love scene,' the Lamb said. 'It's all you ever show us these days.'

'The young lovers are before the tribunal of the high priestess,' the Psammead said. 'The journey is playing out to its end!'

They were inside the office now. It was a large, untidy room, cluttered with books and long sheets of printed paper. Father was stroking his moustache, as he did when agitated.

Anthea and Ernie sat on the other side of the desk. They were all very serious.

'It puts me in a difficult position,' Father was saying. 'I'll have to tell your mother, and – well, it might be tricky, that's all.'

'But you can't object to Ernie because he writes for a living,' Anthea said. 'It's exactly what you do yourself.'

Father smiled painfully. 'My darling, that's why I ought to object – it's a chancy living at the best of times.'

'I wouldn't have asked her to marry me if I wasn't making a decent amount of money,' Ernie said. 'I've got enough to set us up in a home of our own – though I'm staying with Mrs Taylor for the time being.'

'Oh, I know all about your brilliant career,' Father said. 'It's hard to get away from you when the entire world goes round quoting your "Common Soldier" column – including Lloyd George in the House of Commons!' He sighed and sat down at the desk. 'But I'm not thinking like an editor now, I'm thinking like a father. And the fact is that we don't know a thing about your people.'

'I'm not marrying his people,' Anthea said.

'There's nothing much to know,' Ernie said. 'My parents have been gone for years, and I don't know who

288

my grandparents were. All I've got in my favour is that I'll work my fingers to the bone to make Anthea happy.'

'We're not asking for permission,' Anthea said, holding her head up proudly. 'I'm over twenty-one – old enough to make my own decisions. It's just that it would be so much nicer if you gave us your blessing.'

'But he must!' Edie cried out. 'It'll be so beastly if he doesn't – and I want to be a bridesmaid!'

'Good gracious,' the Psammead said faintly, 'my paws are tingling! I shall give the lovers a blessing – as I should have done with Osman and Tulap!' He held his breath and his little body swelled and strained. An invisible change came over the room, as if a mist had cleared or a stone lifted.

'Let's not be dramatic,' Father said. 'Of course I give you my blessing – and so will Mother, when she meets Haywood properly and finds he hasn't got two heads.'

'Thank you, sir,' Ernie said, grinning at Anthea.

'The fact is,' Father said, 'young chaps like you have risked life and limb for your country. The older generation has lost any right it ever had to lay down the law. You go on and be happy, in any way you can – don't listen to us.'

Anthea jumped out of the chair to fling her arms

around him. A shaft of sunlight pierced the grimy windows, until the whole room was a blaze of light, and Edie and the Lamb had to close their eyes against the glare.

★

When they opened their eyes, the Lamb and Edie were a tangled heap of arms and legs on the old sofa in the attic, and it took them several seconds to get free.

'Well, that was a pretty good adventure,' the Lamb said breathlessly. 'The flying was prime – though I could've done with a lot more of it.'

'It was the best adventure ever and I wish we could see them both right now,' Edie said. She reached over to the sand bath to stroke the Psammead's head. 'Are you all right?'

The sand fairy was trembling all over. 'Great heavens,' he whispered. 'My orders have come at last!'

'What do you mean?' She was alarmed. 'Are you ill?'

'Not at all – I feel better than I have done for years! The lovers have been blessed, and I have been forgiven!'

'What are you talking about?'

'I can feel it in my whiskers – I'm about to go home!'

Twenty-four

LAST WILL AND TESTAMENT

'OH, COME OFF IT,' JANE SAID, without looking up from the thick textbook she was reading. 'You're always saying you're about to leave, and you never do. I bet half a crown you're still here next Christmas.'

The Lamb and Edie had brought the Psammead down to Jane's bedroom. She spent most of her time at her desk these days, studying for the first of the exams that would get her into the London School of Medicine for Women. Father's generous cousin Geraldine had offered to pay all the expenses, and – more importantly – managed to make Mother see that Jane wasn't going to change her mind about being a doctor. Edie was pleased to see Jane so happy, yet couldn't help feeling this was yet another of the Bigguns slipping away from them into a private, grown-up world.

'That's a bet you'd lose, Jane,' the Psammead said. 'This time it's really happening. I have the oddest feeling of invisible hands tugging at me.'

'Please don't leave us,' Edie said, for the hundredth time. 'The house will be so sad and horrid without you!'

'I have always appreciated your devotion, Edie, but don't you DARE cry! Jane, stop looking superior. And Lamb, there's no need to curl your lip like that – this time it happens to be TRUE. You really ought to be very pleased for me. I feel the old magic tingling in my fingers again, ready to whisk me away to my long home.'

'I'm sorry, I can't help crying.' Edie scrubbed her eyes on her sleeve; here was the news she'd been dreading ever since the very first day she'd seen the sand fairy in the gravel pit. 'It's just that I love you so much!'

'I know, my dear,' the Psammead said. 'But even your love isn't strong enough to change the workings of the universe. And I feel, deep in my ancient bones, that my transformation is very nearly complete.'

The Lamb and Edie stared silently at the sand fairy, who'd been part of their lives since the beginning of the war, and tried to imagine the White House without him.

'Look here, if it's not another false alarm,' the Lamb said gruffly, 'I'll really miss you, Psammead. Couldn't you wait until we're all together again, so we can say a proper goodbye?'

'No time, I'm afraid,' the Psammead said. 'If sand fairies had suitcases, I'd be packing mine at this minute. Jane, kindly shut that book and find a pen and paper – I wish to dictate my last will and testament, and you have the neatest writing.'

★

'No whispering, please,' the Psammead said. 'This is the solemn occasion of my farewell. Edie, please try to stop crying.'

He had summoned them all to the gravel pit at the bottom of the garden, where he'd made his very first appearance. The weather was dry but the wind was cold; Edie had wrapped her school scarf around his plump body. Lilian was busy digging the tennis court at Windytops into a vegetable garden (the food shortage was getting worse and no one had unpatriotic things like tennis courts anymore; half the lawn at the White House had been given over to cabbages and potatoes), but she had dashed back to lead Robert to the gravel pit.

Robert and Lilian, Jane, the Lamb and Edie stood awkwardly, like mourners at a burial. The Psammead stood on a small hillock, clutching a piece of paper between his paws.

'As you all know,' he began importantly, 'I've been waiting for this moment for years.'

'I thought you still had some more repenting to do,' Robert said.

'More repenting? My dear Robert, I've been doing nothing else since 1914! Just how sorry am I supposed to be?'

'Hmm, I don't know. You don't exactly strike one as a reformed character.'

The Psammead was offended. 'Of course I've reformed! I wouldn't be moving along unless I'd turned myself into a better creature.'

'I know you have,' Edie assured him. 'You're so much kinder than when you first came.'

'Yes,' Jane said, 'that's certainly true. You've learned to consider other people's feelings, which you never did before. But where exactly are you off to now – heaven?'

'I have no idea,' the Psammead said. 'All I know is that the universe is on the move, and I'm going – somewhere.'

Lilian leaned forward to touch the creature's head. 'I haven't known you long – but I think you're adorable.'

'Thank you, Lilian,' the Psammead said. 'Now, if you'll all be quiet, I'd like to read you my will.' He cleared his throat and his telescope eyes turned to the piece of paper. 'This is the last will and testament of the last sand fairy, also known as the Psammead, the Mighty One – and the rest of my hundred-and-eighty titles.

'I don't have any money or property – though several cases of jewellery in the British Museum actually belong to me, and I've marked the numbers on this bit of paper, so that you can steal them back.'

Robert snorted with laughter, which the sand fairy loftily ignored. 'I can only leave a very strong vibration of good feelings and my blessings for the

295

future. You have all been very kind to me, and I'm sorry I didn't have enough magic this time to grant you any decent wishes. Thanks to you children, the concept of "love" now means something to me. If only I'd learned about it sooner, the entire course of history might have been different!

'Time will pass, and memories will fade, but you needn't worry that you'll forget me.

'Who could?

'The Last Psammead.'

In the long silence a bird cawed above their heads.

'Is he still here?' Robert murmured.

'I'm still here,' the Psammead said. 'I'll be on my way any minute now.'

'Are you nervous?' the Lamb asked.

'A little – but mostly excited, as if I were going away on a lovely holiday. I haven't had anything like a holiday for untold centuries.'

'I wish you could visit us sometimes,' Edie said.

'You know that won't be possible – but I can still visit you in your imagination. You must think about me as much as you can.'

'I'll never stop thinking about you!'

'Of course you won't. And wherever I happen to be, I shall miss our after-school chats. But we'd have had to stop them soon, anyway – you'll be leaving Poplar House and going to the high school.'

'Why must everything change?' Edie burst out. 'We were so happy!'

'Because things DO change, whether we like it or not.' The Psammead suddenly held up his paws and stared at them hard. 'My fingers are getting warm – the warmest they've been since I went into hiding! That means the moment of our toodle-oo is imminent.'

'Well, thanks for everything, Psammead,' Robert said. 'It's been a pleasure to know you.'

'Hear, hear!' Lilian said.

'We'll miss you terribly,' Jane said.

'Thank you, Jane. I hope you have a lovely time cutting off limbs when you're a doctor.'

A shudder suddenly ran through the Psammead's body. 'It is upon me! Children – stroke me one last time!'

They all gathered around him and took turns to stroke his little head for the final time. The girls kissed him, and Robert and the Lamb shook his paw.

'Pooh!' snapped the Psammead. 'What are you all doing here? Can't I ever shake you off?'

The gravel pit had been swallowed up in darkness and noise; Lilian, Jane, Edie and the Lamb stared around them. 'What's going on? Where are we?' Robert said.

'If we're following you to your long-term home,' the Lamb said, 'does that mean we're dead?'

'Don't be silly,' the Psammead said, 'of course you're not.'

'I don't feel dead, however that feels,' Lilian said shakily. 'Is this – is this the normal sort of thing that goes on with the Psammead?'

'More or less,' Jane said. 'We're at the front, Bobs, right in the thick of it.'

They were in a trench, so wide and deep that all they could see of the sky was a flashing strip high up between the sandbagged walls. The earth shook, the heavy guns thundered.

The Psammead scuttled along the wooden duckboards at the bottom of the trench, and suddenly dived through a doorway and into a dugout. It was a cramped, dark place that looked as if it had once been the cellar of a house. A gramophone was scratchily playing 'Hitchy-Koo'.

Two soldiers sat writing on either side of a table, by the flickering light of three candles stuck into wine bottles. One of them was Cyril.

Lilian, her eyes round with awe, quickly described the scene to Robert.

'Squirrel looks so old,' Edie said. 'And doesn't he look like Father?'

The other officer was a lot younger, as young as the senior boys at the Lamb's school. The louder explosions made him twitch nervously.

'Pemberton—'

'Hmm?' Cyril glanced up.

'I don't know what to write.'

'It's not a prize essay – just put what you'd want to say to them.'

'What I want to say is too big to put into words.'

'Put that they'll know what you mean,' Cyril said.

The boy took a fresh piece of paper, and they all watched him write 'Dear Mother and Dad, What I want to say is too big—' He sighed and screwed up the paper. 'That just looks idiotic.'

Cyril wrote busily. He had already written two letters, which were neatly sealed beside him. One was addressed to 'Mother and Father, In the event of my death', the other to 'My Esteemed Siblings'.

'They're about to go over the top,' Jane said. 'They're writing letters in case they don't come back.'

'Look, don't worry too much,' Cyril said. 'Ten to one you'll be back to rip it up. I've ripped up dozens of farewell letters in my time. It's a good thing to write them because you feel you've sort of settled everything, and then it all goes to the back of your mind. That's all.'

'Oh, I see,' the boy said, and looked a little less scared.

Cyril went back to his writing. Edie and the Lamb looked over his shoulder to read it.

My darling Mabel,

If you're reading this, it means only one thing – that I've bought it and won't be coming back. I must tell you how much you've meant to me in the few months we've known each other. You're so easy to talk to, and you have just your brother's way of ragging me when I get too gloomy.

I wish I'd been to India – that's where my regiment was supposed to be going, until this war got in the way. I had all sorts of dreams about taking you out there to eat curries and ride on elephants. If it's possible to be a ghost, I'll come and visit you in your garden in Oswestry, among those prize-winning pink roses of yours; you'll feel a slight breeze on the spot below your left ear where I like to kiss you, and that will be me.

Dearest, I hate to think that all I've done is make you sad. For your sake I could almost wish we'd never met – but for my own sake I'm awfully glad we did.

'We shouldn't read any more.' The Lamb's voice was choked. 'He'll be back later to rip it up, just like he said.'

'I say, Pemberton,' the boy said.

'Hmm?' Cyril patiently raised his head.

'Sorry to interrupt again – but is it always like this?'

'What do you mean?'

'The way the waiting seems endless, and you dread it but you're somehow impatient to get on with it, and terrified of bungling the orders—'

Cyril put down his pen. 'Yes, it is always like this.

We all feel just the same about going over the top, even the CO. I won't say you get used to it, but it's a bit better when you know what to expect. You're with Sergeant Bates, aren't you? Stick close to him, do what he says, and you'll be fine. He's a brick and nothing surprises him – he's been in the army since the Wars of the Roses.'

The boy smiled uncertainly. 'Righto. Thanks.'

'Look here, give me a moment to finish my letter, and we'll have a game of rummy.' Cyril smiled in a way that made him look much younger, and much more like himself. 'It's a good way to pass the time and take your mind off the noise, and your winnings may amount to as much as one and six.'

'Typical Squirrel,' Robert said, 'the great cheerer-upper.'

'And you finish that letter to your people,' Cyril went on, 'because it'll worry you if you don't – square up, tell the beggars you love them, then go and find Private Mitchell and tell him to pass round the tea and rum.'

'Yes, sir.' The boy was happier now, and went back to his letter; this time, he knew what to write.

'And so it is accomplished,' the Psammead said.

'Children, hold tight to my paws – the picture is about to change.'

Edie picked up the Psammead and took hold of one of his scraggy little paws. 'Where are we going now?' There was a strange, heavy feeling of dread in her chest, and she could see that the others felt it too; Lilian huddled closer to Robert, and Jane put her arm around Edie's shoulders.

The dugout and Cyril and the young soldier dissolved like a wet painting; the whirling colours resolved themselves into a view of sunlit countryside. Suddenly, they could smell hay and pollen. The Psammead, surrounded by the children and clutching the fingers of Edie and the Lamb, was floating above rich green meadows towards a small town.

On the edge of the town they flew over big houses with large gardens filled to overflowing with summer flowers.

In one garden, a girl stood beside a great cascade of pink roses, with a little black dog cavorting around her feet. The dog looked up at them and began to bark.

'It's Mabel and her dog, Hamish,' Edie said. 'And I think he can see us.'

303

'Stop it, Hamish,' Mabel said. 'What on earth's the matter with you?'

She stopped in the middle of cutting roses and glanced up sharply, letting out a little gasp as her hand touched the spot just below her left ear.

And the picture changed again.

★

The next picture drew together slowly, then they were in a small, bare, white room, like a very clean prison cell. Through the single window they could see red-brick cloisters around a quiet patch of green. In the room was a hospital bed containing a patient almost entirely covered with bandages. A stout nun sat in a hard chair beside him, bent over a book.

'No,' Edie said, 'I don't want to look – please let's go home!'

Jane gently put her hand on Edie's arm. 'It's Cyril.'

'You must look at him!' The Psammead began to tremble in her arms.

Edie had known in the pit of her stomach that it was Cyril. Feeling strangely breathless, as if the world

304

had suddenly stopped, she went to the side of the bed to gaze at his still face.

'It's bad,' Lilian whispered to Robert.

The Psammead jumped out of Edie's arms onto the bed and squatted on the pillow beside Cyril's head. 'Here I am.'

Cyril's eyes opened and his lips twitched into a smile. 'Hello, old boy,' he whispered. 'I knew you'd come.'

The nun carried on reading her book, noticing nothing.

'We're here too, Squirrel,' Edie said. 'Me and the Lamb, and Jane and Bobs and Lilian. Can you see us?'

'Yes,' Cyril said. 'Good of you to visit.'

The Lamb asked, 'What happened?'

'I caught the end of a shell,' Cyril whispered. 'It's made a bit of a mess of me.'

The nun shifted in her chair and turned a page.

'I'm awfully glad you're here. Can you stay with me?'

'Yes, my dear,' the Psammead said and gently stroked Cyril's cheek with his paw. 'I'll never leave you now.'

The Lamb and Edie caught each other's faces, pale and dumb with dread.

'Do they know at home how much I love them?' Cyril asked.

'Most certainly,' the Psammead replied.

'Come on, then,' Cyril said. 'To the next adventure.'

His eyes closed. The deep silence in the room stretched on and on.

The nun glanced up and shut her book. She felt for Cyril's pulse, then made the sign of the cross over him and covered his head with the sheet.

The Psammead's eyes quivered on their stalks, and for the very first time in thousands of years, two large tears formed. For a moment his tears hung like diamonds in the air, and then dropped onto his furry stomach.

'Oh!' he let out a gasp of surprise. 'So this is it – the tears the universe has been waiting for all these years—'

There was a sizzling sound, a little like bacon frying in a hot pan. The Psammead let out a moan – and suddenly nothing was left of him except a heap of soft, golden sand that ran through Edie's fingers when she tried to grab it.

★

They were back in the gravel pit at the White House, as if they'd never been away, staring at each other in breathless silence.

And then they heard the creak-creak-creak of Mrs Trent's bicycle in the lane.

ENGLISH VISITORS ESCAPE ROCKSLIDE

A party of sightseers narrowly escaped serious injury last week, when a pair of ancient desert rocks, known locally as 'Osman' and 'Tulap', suddenly collapsed. 'There was a tremendous rumbling sound,' Dr Banks, an archaeologist leading the tour, said, 'and suddenly the two majestic pillars were reduced to rubble. The natives here are saying that the "lovers" are together at last.'

The Cairo Courier, January 1919

MARRIAGES

On the 25th at St Mary's Church, Bloomsbury, Miss Anthea Pemberton, daughter of Mr and Mrs Charles Pemberton, to Mr Ernest Haywood.

The Times, January 1919

EPILOGUE

LONDON, 1930

'**B**UT – WHY MUMMY?' Polly asked again. 'Why today? Why do I suddenly have to miss a whole day at the farm?'

Anthea turned to look at her daughter. 'Darling, I do wish you wouldn't stop dead in the middle of the pavement every time you make one of your speeches. Can't you walk and talk at the same time?'

Polly started walking again. 'This might be the only nice weather we have for ages.'

'I'm sure it won't be,' Anthea said. 'And you won't notice one day out of two whole weeks.'

'I will, actually – me and the Savages have been making plans for ages.' The 'Savages' was Polly's father's nickname for her cousins, the four rowdy sons of Uncle Bobs and Aunt Lilian. They lived on

311

a large chicken farm in Suffolk, where they ran wild from morning to night, and blind Uncle Bobs terrified the neighbours by driving their motor van across the fields. Visiting them was the biggest treat of the holidays, even nicer than going to the White House to visit Granny and Grandpa. It was very annoying that her mother had suddenly put the visit back another day, and dragged her across London to visit the wrinkled old professor, who never could remember how many years had passed, and often mixed her up with Auntie Edie.

'He wouldn't have telephoned if it wasn't important,' Anthea said. 'He said he'd seen something.'

In the olden days the Professor had lived in lodgings in Bloomsbury, but now he had a house in a posh Kensington square; before Polly was born, he'd written a book with Polly's father about ancient history, which had been surprisingly successful. Polly's father had spent his share of the money on their red-brick house beside Hampstead Heath. Polly's best friend, Joanie, lived two doors down, in another red-brick house. Joanie's mother, Mrs Arkwright, had once been Miss Mabel Harper; now she was interested in 'modern' education, and kept a small school where the children ran barefoot and made mud pies (Polly would have loved to go to this school, but her father said, 'Over my dead body').

Ivy opened the door of the Professor's house. Once upon a time she had been the maid at Old Nurse's, but Old Nurse had died years ago and Ivy had moved to Kensington to live with the Professor as his housekeeper. 'Miss Anthea, dear – bless you for coming so quickly!'

Anthea kissed her. 'How is he? Do you think he's ill?'

'I don't think he's ill, exactly – but something's upset him.' Ivy smiled at Polly. 'He'll be ever so glad to see you. How's that bonny baby brother of yours?'

'We decided to leave him at home,' Anthea said, smiling. 'He's an absolute angel, but he's always breaking things. Those little fat fingers of his get everywhere.'

'He broke two pairs of Daddy's specs in one week,' Polly said.

'Little love,' Ivy said. 'He looks just like your Uncle Hilary.' She began to lead them along the hall and up the stairs. 'The Professor's waiting for you – I've never seen him so agitated.' She knocked on a door and loudly said, 'Mrs Haywood's here, dear.'

313

Polly didn't come here often; the Professor's study was rather grandly furnished, and so stuffed with books and crammed with ancient things that she felt she couldn't breathe. She was always nervous about knocking something over, and the Professor's immense age scared her a little; his wrinkled old body looked as though he was about to fall apart at the seams.

Anthea kissed his fragile cheek. 'Hello, Jimmy.'

'My dear Anthea – and you've brought little Edie!'

'No, darling, little Edie's an old married lady these days – and the author of several rather florid romantic novels. This is my daughter, Polly.'

'Oh – yes – the baby.'

'I'm nine,' Polly reminded him. 'Nearly ten.'

'Oh – yes—'

Anthea pulled a chair up to the desk and sat down near him. 'Now, what is all this?'

The Professor gazed at her and seemed to wake up a little. 'As I told you over the telephone, I saw you! You visited me from the year 1905. You and Robert and Jane – and Cyril—' he pointed with a shaking hand at the rug in front of his desk. 'Standing just there!'

'1905?' Anthea had turned pale. 'Good gracious, I

think I remember – the Psammead gave us one quick wish before tea, and here we were.'

Polly was startled; why was her mother suddenly talking about her old stories?

'I wasn't prepared,' the Professor said. 'And it made me dreadfully sad to see you all, so young and fresh and full of hope! Cyril, with his life before him – and then his death – and all the sorrow came back to me, as if it happened yesterday!'

'I wish I'd seen him too,' Anthea said.

'He did die, didn't he?'

'Yes.' Her voice had the sighing note people made when they talked about the Great War. 'It's awful that we go on getting older, and the dear old Squirrel never does. But he's still with us in a way, when we're all together. And he's still such a part of all our fun – you mustn't think his life was wasted. It was a lovely life, and I know he'd prefer to be remembered in a cheerful sort of way. He's still our cheerer-upper, and he always will be.'

Cyril was the uncle Polly had never known; half the girls at her school had a mantelpiece picture of a dead uncle in uniform. Her eyes strayed around the ranks of photographs that crowded every surface.

Here were her mother and uncles and aunts as round-faced children. There were newer pictures of Anthea and Aunt Edie in their wedding dresses, one of Anthea's paintings, Uncle Bobs and Aunt Lilian and their tribe of boys, Aunt Jane in a group of lady doctors, and Uncle Hilary (formerly the Lamb) in his white barrister's wig. Aunt Jane was a doctor at the Royal Free Hospital on Gray's Inn Road. She wasn't married, and lived with her ginger cat, Tibbles, in a little top-floor flat with a gas ring on the landing, which Polly thought must be heavenly. Uncle Hilary wasn't married either; he said he was still waiting for the girl who could best him in an argument.

'Cyril made the Psammead weep, and through those tears the disgraced god was forgiven,' the Professor said.

'We were glad to know the old Squirrel wasn't alone on his last journey,' Anthea said softly.

Polly was getting more and more bewildered by her mother's behaviour. When she was little, she'd loved the stories about the Psammead, but there was something very odd about the way she was talking about him now. 'That funny little creature – when I remember all the adventures, it's a way of

316

remembering Cyril, and keeping something of him alive.' She caught her daughter's eye. 'Polly, go and ask Ivy to bring up some tea.'

Afterwards, when they left the Professor's house, Anthea was distracted and silent – but Polly had to ask the question that had been bubbling inside her.

'Mummy,' she said.

'Hmm?'

'You were talking about your stories.'

'Stories?'

'About the ancient sand fairy who lived in a tin bath.' She was excited, and a little scared. 'He was real, wasn't he?'

Anthea was startled for a moment – and then she smiled. 'Of course he was real. I never said he was anything else.'

Polly knew she was telling the truth, and her heart jumped with excitement. 'Could you tell me the one about the wings?'

'I thought you were too old and serious for stories about magic.'

'And the one where you wished everybody could be amazingly beautiful.' Polly sighed, dazzled by all the possibilities. 'Oh, why can't the magic come back?'

'But it's never been away,' Anthea said. 'Once it comes into a family, the magic stays forever.'

'How does it stay? Where is it?'

Anthea laughed. 'In the stories, of course – and the special place they have in our hearts.'

'Tell me the one about the Psammead in the pet shop.'

'We'll see.'

And they both ran across the road, to where the pavement was full of sunlight.

AFTERWORD FROM
THE AUTHOR

I FIRST MET THE PSAMMEAD in the late 1960s, when I was eight or nine, in my Puffin Classics edition of E. Nesbit's *Five Children and It*. But the snooty sand fairy was already a lot older than that. He emerged from his gravel pit in 1902, when *Five Children and It* was first published. In 1904 he made a guest appearance in the sequel *The Phoenix and the Carpet*, and in 1906 the five children – Cyril, Anthea, Robert, Jane and the Lamb – met him one last time in *The Story of the Amulet*.

In my story there is another child, Edie, born after the original adventures, and the original children are teenagers and young adults. I've taken all sorts of liberties, but did my best to honour the spirit of those three books and the brilliant woman who wrote them.

Edith Nesbit (born in 1858) was the mother of all modern writers for children. She could do 'realistic' books, such as *The Story of the Treasure Seekers* and *The Railway Children*. But it was her hilarious, imaginative, magical stories that have had the biggest influence on the writers who came afterwards – for instance, there would be no Narnia as we know it if C. S. Lewis hadn't loved Nesbit's books when he was a little boy.

When I read about the five children when I was a child, I saw them as eternal children, frozen for all time in a golden Edwardian summer, like the figures painted on Keats's Grecian urn – 'Fair youth, beneath the trees, thou canst not leave/Thy song, nor ever can those trees be bare.' But what if they walked off the urn and grew up?

The sixtieth anniversary of the First World War fell in 1974, when I was fourteen (this makes me feel as old as the Psammead), and you couldn't turn on the television or open a newspaper without being bombarded with images of this terrible international tragedy. All old people remembered the First World War in those days, and they talked about it to their children and grandchildren because it was so important Never to Forget.

My grandmother (born in 1897) told wonderful stories about being a teenager during the war – often funny, such as the one about Auntie Muriel being chased down the lane by a Zeppelin, but mostly very sad, about the boys she knew disappearing one by one. I remember going to see her while she was in a nursing home, and she was sharing a room with an ancient lady named Miss Ball. Granny told me that Miss Ball had been a nurse at Gallipoli, and that she still cried to remember the sick and wounded men she'd been forced to leave behind when they were evacuated. She wanted me to shake Miss Ball's frail hand, so that I wouldn't forget meeting her, and of course I never have – it was an honour.

Bookish nerd that I was, it didn't take me long to work out that two of E. Nesbit's fictional boys were of exactly the right ages to end up being killed in the trenches – and it was like turning round a telescope to look through the other end. Nesbit was writing at the start of the twentieth century, and her vision of the distant future, as described in *The Story of the Amulet*, was a rather boring socialist utopia. But the chapter of *The Amulet* that most haunted me was the one I have adapted for the prologue of this book, in which the children visit the Professor in the near future – their own future. He knew and I knew, as Nesbit and her children could not, what that future might contain.

When I was young, I saw the First World War from the point of view of the young people who did the fighting. Nowadays I'm old enough to see it through the eyes of the poor parents who lost their boys. In 2012, my darling son Felix died when he was just nineteen, and it's the worst sorrow there is; I couldn't help thinking of all the sad mothers and fathers when I wrote about Cyril, Robert, Harper, Muldoon and the others.

Don't let's forget any of them.

Kate Saunders

ACKNOWLEDGEMENTS

YOUNG CYRIL'S FAVOURITE BOOK, *With Rod and Gun through Bechuanaland* really existed, though I haven't been able to find the author; my father's best friend saw it on the shelf of his very posh mother-in-law and thought it was the funniest title he had ever seen. Thanks, Dad and Bob.

Thanks to my Granny, Marjorie Saunders, who told me how her father used to hang up his long pants instead of a Christmas stocking.

Thanks to Mr Chris Carter for 'Windytops', which was his teenage nickname for his half-timberish family home.

Thanks to my dear friends Eleanor, Jenny and Francesca who let me write them into a novel about the First World War when we were at school; they are still my heroines.

Thanks to Amanda Craig for persuading me to save a character's life at a crucial stage.

Thanks to Alice Swan, my brilliant editor.

Thanks to my family, Bill, Louisa, Etta, Ewan, Ed, Charlotte, Tom, George, Elsa, Claudia and Max.

And thanks to all of you.